Search For Annie

Ron Mahaffey

outskirtspress
DENVER, COLORADO

This is a work of fiction. The events and characters described herein are imaginary and are not intended to refer to specific places or living persons. The opinions expressed in this manuscript are solely the opinions of the author and do not represent the opinions or thoughts of the publisher. The author has represented and warranted full ownership and/or legal right to publish all the materials in this book.

Search For Annie
All Rights Reserved.
Copyright © 2015 Ron Mahaffey
v2.0

This book may not be reproduced, transmitted, or stored in whole or in part by any means, including graphic, electronic, or mechanical without the express written consent of the publisher except in the case of brief quotations embodied in critical articles and reviews.

Outskirts Press, Inc.
http://www.outskirtspress.com

ISBN: 978-1-4787-6064-1

Outskirts Press and the "OP" logo are trademarks belonging to Outskirts Press, Inc.

PRINTED IN THE UNITED STATES OF AMERICA

This book is dedicated to all my friends and family who have encouraged me to continue writing when I was feeling discouraged and cheered me up when I was feeling low.

Other books you will enjoy

ANNIE
THE SECRET

Chapter I

The early October morning, in Colorado, was cool and clear. The brightly shining stars in the night sky still embraced our ranch like a soft blanket. I could see a sliver of morning light starting to eat away the darkness from around the tips of the mountain tops to our east. Annie and I had just finished breakfast and I was sitting at our kitchen table wondering whether or not I had cut enough firewood to get us through the winter. Annie was working around the kitchen completing some of her few remaining, post breakfast, chores while humming a song she must have heard on the radio that was playing softly nearby. I had just made up my mind to cut some more firewood when Annie walked by. My senses suddenly picked up a sweet aroma that reminded me of a perfume I bought her for her birthday. I thought how fortunate I was to have such a beautiful women love such an ordinary man like me. I watched her move with skillful determination from one kitchen task to the next. For some unknown reason to me, she had decided to start tinting her hair blond. I told her I liked it the way it was.

She explained to me, simply, "I just felt like I needed a change."

I must admit that it did bring out those beautiful blue eyes she was blessed with. Watching her move about the kitchen brought back some old memories of the time I watched her move quickly and skillfully around the M.A.S.H unit, in Vietnam, caring for the wounded soldiers. I deeply, to this day, believe if it wasn't for the extraordinary tenderness and loving, skillful care, those nurses gave to our wounded soldiers; many more would not have made it home alive.

It has been a couple of years now since Annie and I had served there but it still only seems like yesterday that it all happened. It's hard for me to believe we have been married for over a year. It seems the older I get the faster time goes by. We've also added to our family, one fine young man who is now the ripe old age of two months. We named him Jim Paul Miller after her father Jim Wilson and my father Paul Miller. We call him by his initials, JP. We hope it will give him a feeling of independence when he gets older. We felt it would also instill pride in both his grandfathers of whom Annie and I, had just learned last year, had met and served together during World War II. They, with Annie's mother, had been spies for the CIA... Or, as it was called prior to and during World War II, the O.S.S... Little did we realize, at that time, how their dangerous past would soon catch up to us and change our future.

I rose from my chair at the table and walked over to Annie. She was standing at the sink washing a few cups and dishes. I slipped up behind her and put my arms gently around her waist softly giving her a hug as I whispered in her ear "I love you."

Just, at that most untimely moment, the phone rang. I reached over to the nearby wall phone and picked it up. "Hello".

I was smiling at Annie and listening to the caller when Annie noticed the expression on my face change to an intense, concentrated look. Annie whispered "What's wrong?"

I continued to listen to the caller for several minutes without saying anything. I hung up the phone and stood there for a few moments, absorbing in my mind, what I had just been told. I looked back at Annie and said "I need to go."

I explained to Annie, as I grabbed my truck keys hanging on the wooden peg next to the front door. "The caller told me that she and her husband had been horseback riding in the mountains. They said I would want to see what they found. The voice said it was crucial information about the disappearance of my parents. They want me to meet with them at the Sand Dunes parking lot in forty five minutes. They said they have evidence that could show where my parent's plane went down."

Annie understood, all too well, my desperate need to find out what happened to my mother and father. It has been eight years now since my parents disappeared in a plane crash. According to the traffic controller it was believed to have disappeared in the Colorado mountain wilderness. It happened during, what should have been a routine flight home from a medical convention in Los Angeles, California.

When I went to leave, I kissed Annie softly, feeling the tender, soft warmth of her lips, which seemed to me, to be pleading for me not to go. I looked lovingly into Annie's beautiful blue eyes and said "I love you and I'll call you from the park's welcome center after I find out what these people have to show me."

I quickly stepped over to the baby bassinet where our eight-week-old son, JP was sleeping and hastily bent down kissing him on the forehead. I quietly whispered in his ear "I love you son." Then turned and quickly ran out the front door.

Annie called out to me "Cody! You forgot your jacket, it's chilly this morning!"

Annie retrieved my jacket from the coat closet near the front door and held it there till I returned. She handed it to me but to my surprise she didn't release it right away. I turned my head around to see what her problem was.

She looked at me with a worried look and said "Be careful Cody."

It seemed like an innocent statement she had made to me several times in the past. This time her worried tone struck me as rather odd and started me thinking about that phone call. I rushed back out the door of our single story ranch home and headed for my truck. The home we lived in had been built in nineteen thirty two by my grandparents. My grandparents were the only family I had left after my parent's possible plane crash and disappearance. It was only eighteen months ago when the terrible freak ranch accident, in the winter of 68 and 69, took both my grandparents lives. Their accidental deaths happened while I had been in a coma due to wounds I received from a bomb explosion while I was in Vietnam.

I quickly climbed into my pickup truck, but my little voice began to trouble me. That little voice in my head was telling me to beware. I thought, beware of what? The phone call from a complete stranger or the tone of Annie's pleading comment? Either way my little voice was trying to warn me something wasn't right. When I was growing up I was always told that I had the stubborn streak of a mule. All these warning alarms going off and I still couldn't talk myself into believing anything was wrong. The eastern sky was getting brighter creating a black rugged looking silhouette of the Sangre De Cristo mountain range that runs north and south along the eastern edge of the San Louis Valley. I normally would have taken time to soak in its beauty but I had a lot on my mind and was in a hurry to arrive at the meeting place on time. I started my pickup truck and backed out of the driveway, but just before I pulled away I turned back to see Annie watching me from the doorway.

I rolled down my truck window and hollered to her "I should be back in two hours." I then pushed the gas petal down, kicking up a lot of dust from our dirt road and disappeared out of sight.

Annie was beginning to worry. She glanced at the clock hanging just above the stove in the kitchen. It was indicating eight thirty and Cody had been gone for nearly two hours. She thought *'Cody should have called by now'*. She began to worry that maybe, something was wrong. He had told her where he was supposed to meet the people and she knew it was only a forty-five minute drive to get there.

Annie was awakened from her momentary thoughts by a knock on the door. She glanced at the clock hanging just above the wall phone, to the right of the kitchen entryway. She noticed it indicated 8:35am and *wondered who could be knocking on her door so early on this beautiful October morning*? She started toward the front door but hesitated for a moment when a thought entered her mind. It has been nearly nine months now since the day she and Cody had their, life altering meeting with her parents. That's when it was revealed, by them, a secret they had been keeping from Annie for nearly thirty years. The secret was that her mother and father had been government agents. They worked for the SIS and OSS during World War II and the CIA after World War II. She remembered clearly her mother and fathers warning to her and Cody *"We still have enemies hunting for us and maybe some of the same enemies might be looking for you and Cody as well."*

She heard a second knock on the door and hollered "Hold on I'm coming!"

Before she answered the door she took one quick look at young Jim Paul Miller, the newest addition to their family, who was still, quietly sleeping in his bassinet in the living room. For just a few moments she stood beside his bassinet looking at him, feeling her heart beat with happiness and enjoying the pure love for the son God blessed her and Cody with.

She stepped over to the side of the living room next to the picture window where she opened the edge of the drape and quickly glanced outside toward the driveway. The only thing she could see was the county sheriff's car parked in the drive. Worry and curiosity started to increase along with her heart rate. Leaving the door's safety chain connected she slowly opened the door just enough to allow her to peek around its edge and verify that it was the sheriff who was knocking. Recognizing the sheriff, she quickly slid the safety chain from the door and opened it. She could feel the coolness of the morning air as it softly brushed against her face and bear arms.

Smiling her warm smile, which amplified her mesmerizing blue eyes, she said "Good morning sheriff what brings you out here so early on this beautiful morning?"

Several miles away, near the town of Alamosa, Colorado, Annie's parents, Jim and Mary Wilson, were at home preparing to leave on their weekly trip into town for supplies. Jim was putting on his jacket while Mary was trying to decide on which would be more practical to wear on this chilly morning, a sweater or perhaps a heavier long coat? Just as she was reaching for her coat the phone rang. Mary stepped over to the wall phone in the kitchen and picked up the receiver. She started to say hello when she heard a terrified voice scream, "MOM THEY FOUND US!" Then the phone went dead.

Jim had been watching Mary as she picked up the phone. He saw her face turn ashen white. Mary set the phone down and looked at Jim. He saw a fear in her eyes he had not seen there for a longtime.

Staring at Jim, she said with a trembling voice, "We need to get over to Anne and Cody's place immediately!"

Twenty minutes later Jim and Mary were driving down the dirt road approaching Anne and Cody's ranch house. As they approached the house they could see the sheriff's car parked in the drive, but didn't see anyone around. When they turned into the drive they saw a body lying on the porch by the front door. Jim instantly stopped the car and reached over to the glove compartment and pulled out the 38 special he kept there for protection. Mary pulled out a semi-automatic 32 from her purse. Nearly thirty years of covert warfare experience and months of on the job combat training instantly went into effect. Both of them knew what needed to be done. Walking cautiously toward the house with their guns up and ready to fire, they carefully approached the sheriff's car.

Mary quickly glanced into the car and after thoroughly scanning the interior said "Clear!"

Jim kept his eyes scanning the single story house and surrounding area for any unusual movements. He had one hundred percent confidence in what he was doing; knowing the love of his life was watching his back. When they reached the porch Jim stepped to one side of the front door while Mary knelt down beside the body and checked for a pulse.

She said "He's still alive Jim."

Jim could see the front door was partially opened. Standing to one side he used his foot to cautiously push the door open the rest of the way. Quickly, he stepped inside and slipped to the right of the door while Mary, with her gun up and ready to fire, entered and stepped to the left. She moved a little further to the left pausing for a few moments scanning the living room and kitchen area for any movement and listened for any unusual noise. Jim started to step further into the house when he suddenly stopped. His sense of smell was warning him about the strong odor of propane gas that filled the room. Mary noticed the change in his movements and knew something was wrong.

With a tone of urgency in his voice Jim said "Gas filled room means only one thing, help me grab the sheriff. Let's get as far away from the house as we can before it blows."

Mary said "What about Anne, Cody, and the baby?"

Jim replied "The basinet in the living room is empty. There was no sign of anyone inside. The coat closet door was open and their coats were gone. I believe whoever did this has all three of them."

Jim and Mary picked up the sheriff by his arms and hastily dragged his limp body off the porch to the rear of their car where they gently laid him down. Mary stayed with the sheriff as Jim rushed to the sheriff's car and quickly started calling on his radio for help, explaining to the dispatcher what the situation was and the need for backup. When Jim returned to Mary he started to tell her help was on the way when he heard a dull thump come from inside the house. A deafening explosion instantly followed, accompanied by a shock wave that blew pieces of the house through the windshields of both cars narrowly missing the three of them as they hid behind their car.

After the initial blast and shock wave had past, Jim checked on Mary and the sheriff and saw they were ok. He then cautiously rose off the ground and peered over the rear of his car toward the house. The house was nothing more than a ball of flame. Whoever did this didn't want to leave any evidence behind.

Chapter II

I was driving east out of Alamosa and glanced to my left, looking out my pick-up truck window, toward the Great Sand Dunes National Park. I was still nearly fifteen miles away, as the crow flies. Even at that distance I could plainly see the light colored sand dunes. They stood out against the, darker colored base of the Sangre De Cristo Mountain range with its, 14,000-foot, mountain peaks. The clear blue sky set off the white, snow covered peaks and the lower elevation, lush green, tundra pines. The bright yellow, fall foliage of the Aspen trees created a beautiful panoramic picture that so few people ever get to see or appreciate.

I started wishing I had brought Annie and JP with me. They would enjoy this natural beauty, but I knew this trip wasn't for pleasure and if my little voice was correct and something did go wrong I didn't want to worry about their safety. The phone caller was a female that said she and her husband had been horseback riding in the Weminuche Wilderness area the week before. She said they had found, what appeared to be a piece from an airplane. She continued toying with my interest by saying they had brought back a small part of the plane's metal fuselage that had a number stamped on it. She added, that she and her husband read in the newspaper that I was willing to pay a reward for any information that would lead to the discovery of the plane. When it comes to money there is always a good chance someone will stoop low enough to come up with a corrupt idea to defraud you. I thought, *'the woman who called said she and her husband would meet me at 8:15am in the parking lot of the Sand Dunes National Park Welcome Center. At that point they would turn over the pieces they had brought back in exchange for the reward'.*

My feeling of excitement, that I may have finally found the information I needed to locate mom and dad's plane crash, was nearly more than I could control. Still though, that little voice in my head kept whispering in my ear. *"Something about this just doesn't seem quite right."*

With the high excitement I was feeling at that moment, my thoughts just couldn't put a finger on what my little voice was trying to tell me.

When I drove into the visitor center parking lot I noticed only three other cars were there. No one was around so I parked my pickup in one of the parking spots close to the entrance and waited for someone to appear. I glanced at my watch that indicated it was nearly 8:10am, thinking I might be a little early I turned on the radio and patiently waited for any sign of my phone caller. The closer it got to 8:30am the more anxious I became. I watched as cars came in and their occupants got out and entered the park. I continued watching people come and go; no one seemed to be looking for me.

When 9am showed up I decided to return home. I was driving out of the parking lot when the local news came on the radio.

The announcer said "We have breaking news that a ranch house in the La Jara area had just exploded. One injury was reported with three missing. Further reports will be coming."

A chill went up my spine as I said "Annie!"

I then realized what my little voice had been trying to tell me all along; this was a trick to get me away from Annie.

I pushed the gas petal to the floor and squealed out of the parking lot. I broke all the speed limits to get home. When I neared my house I spotted Mary and Jim standing by the deputy sheriff's car talking to the deputy. The roar and the dust that my pickup stirred up as it raced toward them alerted them to my arrival. The large cloud of dust I created when I came to a slidding halt just ten feet away, engulfed them, causing all of them to cough and wave franticly to clear the dust away.

Mary's heart jumped for joy when she recognized Cody, who quickly exited the truck.

Mary and I, in panicky voices, asked the same question at the same time, "Where's Annie and JP?"

Instantly the heartbreaking realization of what had taken place began to set in and anger started to build. I started to run towards the pile of burning rubble that had once been our home, but Jim caught my arm and stopped me saying, "They're not here Cody! Mary and I arrived just before the explosion. When we entered the house the smell of gas was strong. I knew it was going to blow any minute so I checked to make sure no one was still inside. I noticed all your coats were gone along with the baby's bag. We grabbed the sheriff's unconscious body lying on the porch and dragged him to a protected area behind our car."

I was in shock as I stood there staring at what use to be our home. I felt as if I was frozen in time, not believing what my eyes were telling me. I continued staring at the burning rubble of our house and wondering how all this could have happened. Who could have done this and why would they do it? Then I started to remember the early phone call that led me away from home. I instantly turned toward Jim and Mary, staring at them with questionable eyes and hearing my little voice telling me this was no accident.

I looked at Mary and could see the tears in her eyes as I asked "It was them wasn't it?"

Jim answered "We believe it was, Anne called us sometime around 8:30 am and her only words were, 'They found us!' Then the line went dead."

The deputy, who was standing quietly listening to their conversation, asked "Who are you folks talking about and why was the sheriff here?"

Jim answered "Deputy, we need to return to your office where I'll be able to explain the situation in confidence. As for your question of why the sheriff was here? I believe he was tricked, by these people, into believing something was wrong at the house. They must have talked him into coming out here to see if Annie was ok. When he knocked on the door and got her to open it they knocked him out and rushed in. It was a pretty good idea, but I need to make a phone call before I will know for sure who may be behind this. When the sheriff regains consciousness I hope he will be able to substantiate some of our suspicions."

The four of us waited as the ambulance, carrying the unconscious sheriff, pulled away. I turned towards the burning rubble and watched the firefighters as they sprayed water on what was left of our burning home. I began to feel that same sick feeling I had felt only once before. It was when I awoke in an Oregon VA hospital, after I was seriously wounded from a bomb explosion at the Non-Commission Officer's club in Vietnam. I had just proposed to Annie when the explosion happened. I spent nearly three months in a coma and another three months thinking Annie had died.

This time I'm feeling double the pain of loss and guilt for not being here to protect Annie and JP. The anger I had not felt for a long time was beginning to build deep inside my soul. It was crying to avenge this evil disaster that started long before Annie and I were born. There was no doubt in my mind that I was going to find JP and Annie. When I do find them, I will end this evil once and for all.

Mary could see the look on Cody's face and knew what he was thinking. She gently touched his arm, startling him out of his thoughts and back into reality.

She looked at him and said "I know what you are thinking and I need you to know that I'm awfully sorry I didn't finish this thirty years ago when I had the chance. I never thought Hilda would survive the war and I just never thought her hatred toward me would last this long and effect all of us this late in life. I promise you, I will permanently end this."

I looked at her and said "Not if I get them first."

Jim was watching the two of them when he interrupted and said "We need to go with the deputy and start searching for Annie and JP. Our car is too badly damaged so Mary and I will ride with the deputy.

Cody, you follow us in your pick-up. Mary and Jim stepped into the deputy's car while I returned to my pick-up. I waited for them to get turned around so I could follow them.

I waited inside my idling pickup until the deputy sheriff was clear of my driveway. Once they cleared the drive I would be able to turn around and follow them back to the sheriff's office. I turned into my driveway to turn around, but stopped for a moment. I watched the firefighters put out the last little bit of flame from the rubble. I looked west and watched Jenny and Jasper, my two pack mules grazing. My Appaloosa horse I had named "Annie" after the love of my life, when I thought she had died in Vietnam, was grazing nearby. Due to insistence from Annie, I changed her name to Lucky. I remembered it was a little over a year ago when I was riding Annie (Lucky) into the mountains to disappear forever and I had paused on a high ridge to rest my animals. The view from the high ridge was magnificent. I looked down from the high ridge toward the blacksmith's ranch, where I just had Lucky's shoes checked. The ranch's appearance nestled in the peaceful mountain valley was pleasing to my eyes. That was when I spotted a rider on another horse leaving the ranch and racing along the same trail I had just come over. I remembered that cougar, that had been tracking me for days. It must have been nearby, because when that horse and rider came near, it jumped out of the trees, scaring the horse who then bucked the rider off and almost over a cliff.

I remembered how ecstatic I was when I rescued the rider and found out it was Annie. I smiled when I remembered Annie's strong request that I needed to change the horse's name. I continued to watch the two pack mules and Lucky grazing among several head of cattle.

I sat in my truck staring off toward the western mountains and whispered to myself "Annie, where are you?"

Just at that moment, I noticed a micro burst of light instantly appear, then disappear, coming from the top of a small hill almost two miles to the west. I remembered, in other similar situations, seeing flashes similar to this. It turned out to be sunlight reflecting off the lens of a rifle scope or a pair of binoculars. I began to think about my conversation with Annie's parents. Mary had said they received a phone call from Annie then the line went dead. It told me whoever kidnapped Annie and JP knew she had completed the phone call for help. Whoever these people were, they couldn't take the chance of being spotted racing down the dirt road heading toward La Jara. The only other way out was going deeper into the mountains which they probably weren't familiar with and probably were afraid they might get lost.

I thought the kidnappers may have only driven far enough west, on the deserted ranch road, to hide out of sight and to watch the ranch until everyone left. Then slowly they would drive back the way they had come giving the impression they were just tourists visiting the mountains. They might then, possibly try to pass themselves off as a normal family who had been out for a day of hiking on the Hot Springs Trail. The trail is located only a few miles further west of this ranch and used by numerous tourists. I thought about driving that direction to see if I could find them. If that flash of light I saw coming from the nearby ridge was the kidnappers watching me, then I could be endangering the lives of Annie and JP. I quickly dismissed the thought of going that direction.

Instead, I decided my best bet and safest course of action would be to drive two miles east to the small town of Centro. It was a small village with a few homes and farms located a couple miles east of here. Doing it that way would give, whoever was watching, the impression I was following the deputy back to La Jara. I backed out of my driveway and headed east following the same route the deputy had gone. While I was driving east I remembered a long storage barn sitting close to the road just past the outskirts of Centro. When I arrived at its location I quickly turned off the road and drove around the barn to its southeast corner and parked. Sitting in this location I knew cars driving from west to east wouldn't notice me. I put my truck in park, turned the engine off and waited patiently, praying my theory was correct.

Chapter III

Two miles to the west of her home Annie sat in the backseat of a black Chevy van with heavily tinted windows, holding JP who, so far, was sleeping peacefully. One of her kidnappers sitting in the front seat had turned partway around so he could keep an eye on her. The other two were laying on the top edge of a small ridge, using a pair of binoculars, watching what she believed was her home. So far, none of them had said anything to her, but she did recognize the German language when they talked to each other. Her mother could speak French and German fluently but Annie only understood a few words of it. She had taken a course in Latin that was required for her nursing license but that's where her language training stopped. Now she was wishing she had learned more.

She heard a boom that was so loud the power of it caused the van to shake from its concussion. The two men lying on the ridge let out a loud cheer and gave each other a high five. The driver of the van, who was watching her, gave her an evil grin. She instantly realized the explosion must have been her ranch house blowing up. She thought of her mother and father, whom she had called just as the kidnappers were breaking into her home. Anger was replacing her fear as she realized that her parents may have been at the house. She was also worried about the sheriff, whose unconscious body was still lying on her porch after he tried unsuccessfully to fight off the three men trying to attack her. He fought heroically giving Annie enough time to call for help. The three men overpowered him, knocking him unconscious, then kicked the front door in and forced her and JP into their van. She angrily glared at the man watching her from the front seat. She figured him to be in his mid-fifties or early sixties with black hair, lightened on both sides of his head with a touch of gray. His dark brown eyes were surrounded with deep wrinkles and displayed a tired look that comes from lack of sleep.

She didn't care if he understood her or not as she said "You people have just made a huge mistake. You have just opened a Pandora's Box and it's only a matter of time before all of you are caught!"

An angry look came onto the man's face as he said "You will be there when this ends. You're the bait we needed to catch and kill the two spies who helped to destroy the fatherland. We eliminated one of the spies, now that we have you, we will soon destroy the other two."

Annie had a good idea who he was talking about when she replied "So Hilda Mueller is still alive."

A shocked look came across his face as he asked "So you know about my wife?"

Up to this point Annie was only guessing, but now she knew for sure and could feel fear trying to replace her anger. There was no way she was going to let this big baboon enjoy his intimidation. She kept her angry look of loathing aimed toward him until the other two men returned from the ridge. The older man, who climbed into the front seat with the driver, seemed to Anne, to be in his late twenties or early thirties. He had brown hair and displayed enough genetic details that Annie felt sure he had to be the drivers son. His physical features she felt was young in appearance but the deep creases around his eyes indicated to Annie, he had a lot of years dealing with stressful situations. The second man, she estimated to be near her own age, climbed into the backseat where he sat down beside her. He had blond hair and blue eyes and displayed similar genetic qualities as the other two men giving her the confidence in thinking all three men were related. The young man sitting next to her had an arrogant attitude which she felt must be typical of any German descendant who was influenced by the Nazi ideology.

His blue eyes were cold and calculating. He gave her the feeling that he was evil and would not hesitate to kill her and JP on the spot

After the two men got in the van, the driver turned the van around and headed back toward the ranch. When they approached Annie's home she was shocked to see nothing was left standing. The firemen, who had finished putting out the blaze, had left. She spotted the sheriff's car still sitting in the driveway and noticed how badly damaged it was. She was stunned when she saw her parents' badly damaged car parked behind it. Her heart sank as she wondered if her mother and father had been wounded or killed in the explosion. She didn't see Cody's truck and assumed he was ok and hadn't returned from his meeting at the Sand Dunes Park. Seeing the amount of damage to her parents' car deeply worried her. They continued their drive down the dirt road, heading to the main highway. Annie kept looking around for any sign that might give her a glimmer of hope that help was on the way. Hope came to her when they drove through Centro and Annie just happened to glance toward the storage barn on the right hand side of the road.

Her heart started racing when she spotted Cody's pickup parked near the back southeast corner of the barn. The other three didn't notice it because they were concentrating on the road ahead. She took a quick glance back, one more time, and saw his truck start to move out. A tremendous relief came over her, but she realized that she needed to hide her feelings so her kidnappers wouldn't notice. When they made their right turn onto the main highway going south, she took one last look over her right shoulder and could see the dust cloud Cody's truck was making. She knew he would follow them to the ends of the earth in order to get her and JP back.

Traveling south, Anne knew they would be driving by the sheriffs' office. She watched as they approached and drove by the office. She was hoping to see something that would indicate her parents were ok. When the van sped by she caught a glimpse of a person looking at them from the sheriff's office window. She recognized the face her heart jumped for joy as she thought... *'IT WAS MOTHER!'* She began to feel a little bit at ease knowing her mother was ok and felt her father was probably there with her making plans for a search and rescue. She knew it was only a matter of time now before this ended. Her tensions eased a bit realizing her parents were safe and Cody was following close behind. She knew he would never give up until these clowns were caught. She looked up and spotted the van driver looking at her through his rear view mirror.

He gave her a sinister grin and said "We know that your parents were back there at the police station.

Martin saw them leave your place in the sheriff's car. You can keep hoping for them to come after you, but until we are ready for them, they will not get you back."

Annie didn't say anything; she now knew her parents were ok and the name of one of her kidnappers. She smiled inside and held tightly to JP knowing that these idiots had no idea Cody was following close behind.

Chapter IV

Twenty minutes had passed with no cars driving by; I watched as the fire trucks drove by and disappeared down the road in a cloud of dust. Ten more minutes passed and I was beginning to worry that my theory was wrong.

Time was running out and I needed to be at the sheriff's office in fifteen minutes. I was reaching for the ignition key to start my truck and head for the sheriff's office, when suddenly a fast moving black van went by. The windows were tinted dark so no one would be able to see inside. I was beginning to feel more confident about my theory. The black van that sped by must be the one carrying Annie and JP. No one I knew drove a van and I had lived here for eight years with my grandparents and knew everyone within twenty miles. I started my truck and pulled out from the barn turning right to follow the van at a safe distance. I was aware that if I were spotted by the kidnappers they would probably kill Annie and JP immediately and dump their bodies beside the road.

I watched as the black van came to the end of the road and stopped. I thought they would turn left and drive towards Alamosa, but was surprised when they turned right taking them south towards New Mexico. I kept a safe distance from the van as it pulled out onto the paved road. Slowly, I approached the stop sign and patiently waited until the black van was far enough away so they wouldn't notice me turning their direction. I pulled out onto the paved road and started slowly increasing my speed so I wouldn't lose sight of them. Going this direction would take me right by the sheriff's office where I knew my in-laws were talking with the deputy. I knew one of them would be watching out the sheriff station window wondering where I was at. This would give me the opportunity to do something that would draw their attention. I had to be sure that, whatever I did; would not draw the attention of the van carrying Annie and JP. When I approached the sheriff's office I could see the deputy's car parked out front so I laid heavily on the horn until I drove by.

Inside the sheriff's office Mary was watching out the window wondering what had happened to Cody. Jim was explaining to the deputy what the situation was and showing the deputy his government credentials.

Watching out the window for Cody, Mary saw the black van drive by, but didn't think much of it until she saw Cody's pickup truck approach. She watched, thinking he would turn in, but was surprised when he drove by honking his horn and pointing south. Remembering the black van that drove by only a few moments earlier, Mary suddenly realized what Cody was trying to tell her.

She turned to Jim and quickly said "Jim, Cody just drove by following a black van; he was honking his horn and pointing straight ahead. I think he might be following the kidnappers. Both vehicles are traveling south."

Jim turned to the deputy and said "Deputy we need to follow that pickup!"

The deputy responded "Yes sir, let's go."

All three of them rushed out of the office and into the cruiser. The cruiser's tires spun gravel as the deputy raced out of the parking lot onto the paved road. He picked up speed and started to turn on his siren and flashing lights when Jim reached over and stopped him.

"Deputy, we need to maintain silence, we don't want the kidnappers to know we're following. If they see us they may kill their hostages,"

The deputy, feeling a little embarrassed for not having thought of it himself, agreed with Jim. The deputy called on his radio for the dispatcher as he pressed

SEARCH FOR ANNIE

down on the gas pedal to catch up with Cody.

He told the dispatcher to notify the New Mexico State police to watch for a black van heading south, on highway 285, leaving Colorado.

He said "Betty, make sure you tell them not to intercept just keep track of it and to stay out of sight. This is a kidnapping of a mother and her baby. We don't want to get anyone hurt. Call the FBI and inform them of our situation!"

The dispatcher replied "Copy that Tom, I'll let them know."

Trying to keep my distance, but not too far behind, I was following the black van as they passed through Romeo and headed to Antonito, Colorado. Antonito is a small community with a population of around 700. It has a tourist attraction that draws a lot of people, every year, from around the world. The scenic Cumbres & Toltec Railroad is a late nineteenth century steam driven locomotive. It pulls several passenger cars designed and decorated in the décor of the late eighteen hundreds. Passengers ride on a six hour train ride through the mountains where they are rewarded with breath taking views. The trip starts in Antonito, Colorado and ends in Chama, New Mexico.

I estimated I was only six and a half to seven miles

from Antonito. After Antonito there wouldn't be any more towns all the way to the New Mexico border. Once you cross the border, there wasn't another town for thirty miles. I was trying to figure out what their next move might be.

I thought 'If these people are who I think they are I believe they won't harm Annie or JP until they can do it in front of Annie's mother, aka, Maria Annette Marceau. A year ago she surprised Annie and I when she revealed to us she had been a French spy during the early years of World War II.

I smiled when I thought of my mother-in-law being a spy. Her natural friendly manner could easily fool the wisest of men and penetrate the hardest of hearts, causing them to reveal their deepest secrets. No wonder the Nazi's still have a reward out for her, wanting her dead or alive.

I looked into my rearview mirror and could see, what I hoped would be, the La Jara deputy sheriff's car closing in from about a mile back. I was entering the city limits of Antonito, Colorado and decided to close the distance between me and the black van. To my surprise, the van slowed down and turned left into the Cumbres and Toltec Railroad station parking lot. My mind began to wonder why? They wouldn't be stopping here just for a train ride into the mountains, would they? There had to be something more to it.

SEARCH FOR ANNIE

I slowly followed their lead turning left off the main highway and into the parking lot. I was trying my best not to be noticed as I nonchalantly parked in a spot four rows away from the black van. I watched two men exit the van, one from each side of the front seat while a third came out of the side cargo door, which was the exit door for the backseat passengers. The man who exited the driver's side was, by my estimate, about five foot nine and weighed approximately 190 lbs. He wore a blue denim jacket with blue jeans whose pant cuffs were tucked into his shiny cowboy boots. I slightly smiled as I remembered, the last time I had seen a man tuck his blue jeans into his cowboy boots was back in the fifties. I was watching the top three western cowboy shows on television, at that time, Hopalong Cassidy, the Lone Ranger and Roy Rogers. The man I was watching also had black hair and looked like he was in his late fifties or early sixties.

I watched him walk around the van and stand by the opened cargo door. My heart leaped for joy when I saw Annie exit with JP in her arms. I wanted to jump out of my truck and race over to her, but I kept control of my feelings. I knew, all too well, that if I tried anything here in the train station parking lot, the kidnappers would not hesitate to kill all of us. I thought I would have a better chance where there were more people around to witness what was going on. I felt the kidnappers might think twice before causing an incident that could ruin their plans and disappoint their boss; plus, I also felt that if I tried to do anything by myself I might lose the opportunity to rescue Annie and JP.

After they had passed the sheriff's office none of the kidnappers had said anything to Annie during the rest of the trip down to Antonito. When they arrived at the train station Adolf pulled into the parking lot and parked the van two rows from the entrance to the depot. He exited the van leaving the keys in the ignition knowing he wouldn't need them anymore. He told Martin and Herman to get out. Annie started to worry about what was going to happen when she looked out the van's window and saw Cody's truck drive in and park four rows away. Herman opened the cargo door and stepped out.

He turned to Annie and said in his stern German accent "Fraulein, if you don't want to see your baby die you will not make us any trouble, verstehen?"

Annie understood enough German to know what he said and nodded her head in agreement.

All four of them, with JP in Annie's arms, walked towards the train station. Annie nonchalantly glanced around the parking lot and spotted Cody's truck. She

SEARCH FOR ANNIE

could see him sitting in the truck watching them. She felt a great relief knowing he was close by, but at the same time, she was hoping he wouldn't try anything yet.

She said to the kidnappers "I've never been here before where are we?"

The van driver replied "Don't worry about it. You won't be here that long and if you are thinking of some kind of trick that might get you help, remember your baby's life depends on your behavior. We don't want trouble; we just want your mother. "

I watched as the group entered the train station. When I exited my pickup I noticed the La Jara, Colorado Deputy Sheriff's car pull into the parking lot. The deputy, trying to stay hidden from the depot's front entrance, parked his car between two other pickups. He felt it would hide the, SHERIFF, decal that is printed on each side of the car. Keeping low and dodging from one vehicle to the next, I quickly approached the deputy's car and started telling the three of them that I had spotted Annie and JP with three of the kidnappers.

I quickly told them, "They entered the train depot making it appear as if they might be taking the train somewhere. Annie knows I'm here, I saw her look directly at me. I'm going to go into the station and buy a ticket, like any ordinary tourist would do. Then I'm going to follow them until I find the best time to act."

Jim spoke, "Cody, Mary and I have come up with a plan and we feel it will work, but we need you to remain hidden until we make our move. Mary and I know who is behind this and the sooner we get to her the sooner we can end this. So stay close but not to close. We're counting on you to jump in and pull Annie and JP to safety when trouble begins."

Mary reached through her open rear seat window and placed her hand on Cody's arm and said "I know that when this situation comes to a head you'll get my daughter and grandson out alive. No matter what happens, get them out! One way or another Jim and I will make sure this never happens again!"

Jim handed the deputy a slip of paper and said "Call that number and ask for Sam Young. Tell him who you are and that we're following the kidnappers. Tell him we believe their taking the Cumbres and Tultec Railroad to Chama, New Mexico. He'll take it from there."

Thomas Kinkade has been a deputy with the LaJara sheriff department for nearly five years now. His five foot eleven inch height, hazel eyes and sandy colored hair with a, roughly, two hundred pound muscular physic would make any stranger think he was an

Olympic athlete. He had been hoping for an exciting case like this to come along. Now that he had one, he wasn't about to quit just yet. He turned to Jim and said "Sir, I'll call this message into my dispatcher and follow you until this gets out of my jurisdiction."

Jim looked at the deputy and could see the excitement of the chase in him "Ok deputy go ahead and call it in, then meet us inside the station."

I heard what my father-in-law had said to the deputy. I didn't feel we should all show up entering the station at the same time, so I said "I'll see the three of you on the inside." Casually, so I wouldn't draw attention, I headed for the ticket counter.

When I entered the train station I carefully scanned the crowd of tourists who were waiting anxiously to board the train. Doing my best performance as a tourist, I calmly walked over to the ticket booth and purchased a coach ticket. I mingled with the crowd while searching the area trying to locate Annie. I spotted her and the three kidnappers standing at the farthest point down the train platform near where the parlor cars are located. I thought, *'Now would be a good time to rescue Annie and JP. I don't believe they would try anything in a crowd of people. If they did try anything in the way of violence they knew some of the people standing around would try to help. If the kidnappers tried to fight back it would definitely bring in the police.'*

I thought, *'I'm going to casually walk over to her and using a diversion I'll grab Annie and JP. By the time the kidnappers realize what happened I'll have them safely away.'*

Just before I started to make my move a hand touched my shoulder causing me to turn sharply ready to fight. It was Jim, dressed in a train conductor's uniform. I was amused to see my father-in-law dressed as a train conductor. I wondered how he had obtained the outfit, until I remembered he had been a top CIA agent for many years. His experience gave him several ideas on what he needed in order to blend into any situation.

"Hold on Cody, we don't want anyone to get hurt. Mary and I have a plan that we feel will work and prevent innocent people from getting involved. So, if you will trust us and do what we ask, we'll soon have Anne and JP safely back with you. OK? All we ask is that you let us take the lead in this and do what we ask."

"Yes sir, for now I will, but if I see something going wrong I'll do what I need to do to save Annie and JP, regardless of who gets hurt, including me."

Jim, feeling pride for this young man, replied "I understand. Now this is what I need you to do."

Chapter V

The train whistle blew and Jim, playing the part of the conductor, hollered out "ALL ABOARD! Train now loading for Chama, New Mexico. All passengers climb aboard please."

Jim assisted some of the passengers up the train steps as he watched the three kidnappers escort Anne and JP into the last car of the train. The parlor car, which usually is used by tourists who needed a little more privacy, is furnished with late 1800 decor. The train whistle blew again to let everyone know it was ready to pull out. Jim took one last look around and waved to the engineer, letting him know everyone was on board and it was safe to go. When the train jerked and all the cars rattled into movement he jumped onto the train car platform and entered the first tourist car, asking for tickets. Then he exited the rear door of the first car and entered the second tourist car as he slowly worked his way to the parlor car. He knew he was taking a big risk and was hoping his real identity wasn't known to the three kidnappers.

When he entered the parlor car he noticed the steward was walking around to each passenger asking if there was anything he might be able to get for them. Jim counted five couples, plus Anne, JP, and the three kidnappers which added up to fifteen people in the car. The timing was not yet right for a rescue. While keeping one eye on Anne, who was feeding a bottle to JP, he started asking the rest of the passengers for tickets. He slowly worked his way through the train's parlor car approaching Anne's position.

Anne felt a great relief and a bit amused when she looked up and saw her father in a conductor's uniform. She knew that Cody must be nearby. She looked back down at JP, who was happily sucking away on his bottle totally oblivious to the dangers around him. Anne hoped none of her kidnappers noticed any unusual movements that she might have unknowingly made. She felt nothing she had done should have drawn the kidnapper's attention. She glanced around at the three men sitting with her and noticed them watching the conductor. Trying to draw their attention away from him she asked "Where do we go from here?"

The young, blond, blue eyed, man who had been sitting next to her in the van replied in an arrogant attitude "You'll find out when we get there."

Not looking up from JP she sensed her father

approaching and heard him say "Good morning gentlemen, may I see your tickets please?"

Each of the three men handed him their ticket, which he punched and handed back to them. Then he said "and yours miss?"

Anne looked up into his eyes. There was no detection of recognition from him and none from her. Anne started to say something when one of the kidnappers interrupted.

Speaking, with a distinctive German accent, the man who had been driving the van and claimed to be Hilda Mueller's husband said "Herr Wilson, es ist gut to finally meet you. If you don't want injury to come to your daughter and grandson I suggest you sit down."

Jim, trying to maintain his cover said in a calm voice "Sir, I believe you have me mistaken for someone else."

"No I haven't Herr Wilson my wife, Hilda Mueller, remembers you very well. She has had your description and a hand drawn sketch of you for a longtime now. She is most eager to see you again, especially Maria. Speaking of her, where is she? I hope she's not trying anything funny. I would hate to disappoint my wife by shooting you three right now. So please, have a seat while we wait for Maria to make her appearance. Martin! Search him carefully."

The middle aged young man, who stood about 5ft 9in with black hair and brown eyes, appeared in good physical condition. He was seated to the right of Anne.

He stood up without causing any disturbance and casually searched Jim. He found the 38 special Jim had hidden in the inside coat pocket of his conductor's uniform. He carefully removed it then slipped it under his own jacket. When he had finished his search he quietly whispered to Jim "sit down!"

Jim sat in the empty chair next to Anne, which Martin had abandoned when he got up to search him.

Jim knew his part of the scheme was working. He was now close enough to Anne that he could protect her and JP when trouble started. Jim needed to find answers to several questions. Slyly he started directing questions toward the man who had just searched him asking, "You must be Hilda's oldest son, am I right?"

The young man didn't say anything; he just looked over at the older man who seemed to be in charge. Jim looked at the older man also and said "Alright let me guess."

Looking at the older gentleman Jim said "I think you're the father of these two younger boys and I believe you are Hilda's husband, but what is your real name. I don't believe any self-respecting Nazi would use his wife's last name as his own. That would be like a child hiding behind his mommy's skirt."

The older gentleman's face was turning red. With a sound of bitter arrogance in his voice he said "Sahr gut Herr Wilson, your judgment has not diminished with your old age. Ok, I'll play along until Maria decides to

SEARCH FOR ANNIE

show herself. My name is Adolf Kessler, you of course remember my father Major Kessler. The two young men here are my sons, Martin, the oldest, and Herman, our youngest. We have been hunting for you for thirty years. Now we finally have you where we want you. Once we get to where we are going I will take great pleasure in assisting my wife when she eliminates two more spies who helped to destroy the powerful Aryan Nation!"

Jim knew from years of experience if you insult a person's pride with your questions it will make them angry, causing them to reveal more information. Jim kept up his questioning, irritating his captors with each sentence.

Jim asked "Now that we know who wears the pants in the family, or maybe I should say, the dress in your family, where are you taking us?"

Adolf, by Jim's estimate, was somewhere around fifty-five to sixty years old, 5 feet 11 inches tall and weighed approximately 220 lbs. He had black hair mixed with shades of gray. His bright red face was showing his obvious hate and anger toward Jim. Jim seeing the hatred in Adolf's eyes asked "You say you have killed two other spies? That wouldn't have been my good friend Paul Miller and his wife, would it?"

Adolf's face instantly went from anger to a calm satisfaction as he said "Yes!"

Chapter VI

Several seats away sat Mary disguised as an elderly lady. She was wearing an old light blue winter coat that hung down to her ankles. She kept herself slightly bent over to give the appearance of being physically troubled and needing to walk with a cane. She listened closely to the quiet conversation going on only a few seats away. She was writing the captors names and information down on a small piece of paper. Her true appearance was hidden by the heavy use of make-up and wearing a colorful silk scarf she had hurriedly purchased at the train station. The ankle length coat she had put on earlier that morning, just at the exact moment she received Annie's frightening phone call. The coat added perfectly to her disguise. She was escorted onto the train by the La Jara deputy, Thomas Kinkade. He also changed out of his uniform and into a pair of blue jeans and a light brown jacket. The jacket helped to conceal his 9mm pistol. He had escorted Maria, playing the part of the elderly woman, to her seat and

SEARCH FOR ANNIE

sat down next to her, giving everyone in the train car the impression he was her son.

Annie's face didn't reveal the anger that rose from deep within her when she heard Adolf say, yes to killing Cody's parents. She slowly glanced around the train parlor car hoping to locate Cody but she didn't recognize anyone. She began to wonder if Cody had even gotten on the train. A few seconds later the parlor car door opened and the steward walked in carrying a tray of complimentary drinks for everyone in the car. The steward worked his way through and around the passengers, offering everyone a drink as he slowly approached the little group that surrounded Annie. Annie tried hard to contain her amusement when she recognized Cody in the steward's uniform. The black pants and shoes with a white shirt and black vest; made for her, a humorous sight. She was beginning to feel a bit safer, knowing her father was beside her and her husband was close by.

Anne inquisitively asked Adolf "Was it you who called my husband early this morning and told him you had information about his parents missing plane?"

Cody, portraying the perfect train steward, listened intently as he handed each of them their drinks and turned to walk away. He stopped by the elderly lady's seat and slowly handed her and her son their drinks just as Adolf replied to Annie's question.

"No, that was my wife's idea to get you alone. We didn't need him getting in our way so my wife sent him on what I believe you Americans call, a wild goose chase. We wanted him far enough away so he wouldn't have time to return home in case our plan didn't work out. Hilda told him she would meet him at the Sand Dunes National Park with new information about his parents."

Annie continued "Where is your wife? Why isn't she here to greet us? How disrespectful of her. Any normal person would have been here to personally greet us themselves."

Martin Kessler clinched his fist as he showed his hateful resentment toward Anne's string of questions. He leaned forward in his seat and replied in a low evil tone "My mother will greet you soon enough and while she deals with your mother, I'll be teaching you some German respect!"

Anne could see the pure hatred in his eyes as the cold chill of fear returned to her. She felt her father's hand touch hers and turned to look at him. He didn't say anything but she could read his look and understood its meaning. She had learned the meaning of that look while growing up. Whenever she was getting too vocal towards her mother or stepping out of line with him, she could see the look in his eyes that clearly said to back off and settle down or trouble would soon

SEARCH FOR ANNIE

follow. Even though she could see that same look this time, this one came with a loving smile.

I was only a short distance away when I heard Annie's comment and Adolf's answer. Even though I kept my cool, my insides wanted to react intensely toward Adolf, but I knew now wasn't the time. I was working really hard at trying to maintain my composure. My white knuckles, tightly gripping the tray I was holding, began returning to a normal color. I looked at Mary as she carefully removed a drink from my tray. Her look of calm demeanor helped me to control my own feelings as I finished serving the remaining passengers in the car and then quietly walked out.

The train's whistle blew, echoing its deep, resonating sound, up and down the mountain pass. The engines heavy sounding chug, chug, chugs, could be clearly heard from the open air car where most of the passengers had gone. The open air car, called the gondola, provided the passengers with unobstructed scenic views of the surrounding snowcapped mountain peaks. Only a few of the elderly passengers remained in the parlor and tourist cars. Jim and Mary had taken this trip recently, but only as tourists, giving them a somewhat slight advantage over the kidnappers. Jim was familiar with its travel route and knew their first short stop would be the old lava tank where they would add water. It was needed for the boiler and the long climb up the steep grade to Osier Dining Hall. Once they reach the dining hall the train would stop for lunch. Jim could see Mary and the deputy sitting several seats away. Before the train left the station he asked the deputy to get a message off to Sam Young in Washington. He also hoped that when the local police found the deputy's car in the train station they would figure out everyone was on the train. By now, the sheriff in La Jara, may have regained consciousness and hopefully sent out an all point's bulletin alerting surrounding law officers of the trouble.

Jim knew that once the authorities figured out where they were, then authorities would have the Chama, New Mexico train station covered by agents when the train arrived. The problem Jim was worried about was the local authorities showing up in uniform. If they did, then his chance of catching Hilda would be lost. He prayed that with Hilda's capture, decades of espionage and murder would finally come to an end.

Back in Washington D.C., at the C.I.A. headquarters, Jim's old friend, Sam Young, had just completed dictating a memo to Melissa, his secretary of nearly ten years. His phone rang. Sam, sitting at his desk turned slightly in his swivel chair and picked up the phone answering "Sam here, what can I do for you?"

SEARCH FOR ANNIE

His relaxed position suddenly stiffened as he sat up listening intently to whoever was on the other end of the phone. Melissa's apprehension increased dramatically as she watched him quickly stand up from his chair.

She listened as Sam said "How long ago? Who made the call? He quickly hung the phone up and with a tone of urgency in his voice he said "Melissa! Get me Michael Sean in research and see if you can get hold of Tim Walker and Henry Steel. Tell them we have a code red in Antonito, Colorado!"

A few minutes later Michael Sean entered Sam's office in a hurry. "Sir, you asked for me?"

Michael was a medium build, blue eyed, 5foot 8 inch tall, thirty two year old young man with light brown hair and a degree in criminology from the University of Tennessee. He had started working for Sam and the C.I.A eleven years earlier. On a whim, Mike decided to visit the C.I.A headquarters during spring break of his senior year of college instead of partying on some over populated beach. He felt, doing it this way, would put him a jump ahead of the competition who might be looking for the same job. On the day he visited the C.I.A. headquarters the company was holding their annual recruiting day interviews. Mike thought, *'the timing couldn't have been any better. Most of our life we get fed bitter pills we're expected to take without complaining. Every once in a while we get the opportunity to grab for the gold ring. My time for the gold ring is now, so why not?'*

By pure coincidence Sam was his interviewer and was impressed with Mike's knowledge of criminal history and his deductions of what had transpired on several cases. Sam offered him the job of research analyst and Mike excitedly accepted the position.

Sam looked up from his desk at Mike, "Mike! I need you to pull up all the case files on Hilda Mueller from May of 1940 to present. We have a foreign presence in our country that has kidnapped two of our agents. I need all the information you can get me in the next five minutes."

"Yes sir! I'll get right on it." As Mike raced out the door he hollered back "I'm going to grab Buddy to give me a hand."

Sam stopped for a moment and looked up from his desk watching Michael race out the door. He smiled with pride knowing he was the man who hired Mike and also knowing Buddy had been a down and out street orphan that Mike and his wife, Maggie, had been raising. They found him, twelve years ago, at the ripe old age of eleven, trying to stay out of the cold wind by hiding inside the Lincoln Memorial. Buddy was now one of the company's top part time assistants with one more semester of college, studying criminology, to

SEARCH FOR ANNIE

complete before he graduated.

Sam yelled! "Melissa! Have you gotten in touch with Henry or Tim yet?"

"Yes sir, there in Santa Fe and said they will be in Chama in five hours to meet the train when it arrives."

Sam replied "Tell them to forget the station and ask for the local authorities for their assistance in getting a helicopter to follow the train. Be sure they know to stay far enough away so they don't raise suspicion from the kidnappers. Then, get me the FBI."

"Yes sir, I'll do it right away."

Sam added quietly "Melissa, one more thing, get me MI-6 in London."

Chapter VII

The train had reached its highest elevation when it went through the Cumbres Pass at 10,015 feet above sea level. Now it began its long descent in elevation until it reached its final destination in Chama, New Mexico. Jim realized the trains ride had only thirty more minutes left until it ended. He had to find out what the kidnappers next move would be, so he started probing Adolf for more information.

Jim looked over at Adolf and said, with a little sarcasm in his voice, "So Adolf, where will we be meeting your lovely wife?"

Adolf replied in an angry whisper "Herr Wilson, you will find out when we get there. Until then, keep your mouth shut or I'll do it for you!"

Jim responded, "Now Adolf, you know as well as I do, if you do anything to me right now these people will alert the local authorities. Afterwards you and your sons would be spending the rest of your lives in an American prison."

SEARCH FOR ANNIE

Adolf grinned and replied "Maybe so Herr Wilson but you and your daughter and grandson won't be alive to enjoy it."

I was at the other end of the car carrying a tray full of cookies and candy for the passengers who wanted some sweets and snacks. I was helping the elderly tourists, which in turn, allowed me to keep a close watch on Annie and JP. It also kept me from drawing attention to myself. The white, porter's shirt with the black vest and the black dress pants I was wearing, gave me the appearance of a normal employee. I had acquired the uniform from the real porter for fifty bucks back at the train station. I explained to him what was going on and he was more than happy to sell me his uniform and agreed to stay out of sight. My patience was wearing thin as I continued to wait for a sign from Jim or Mary when to move in. The deputy sitting next to Mary was feeling the same restlessness.

He wanted to move in, but Mary kept him calm as she whispered "Easy Tom, we don't want to scare the little fish off until we get a chance to reel in the big one."

Thomas Kinkade had just reported for duty that morning when the call came in, around 8:55am to the dispatcher about the kidnapping and explosion at the

Miller's ranch. I looked at my watch for the time. It showed 2:40 pm, I knew the end of the ride would be soon. I looked at the deputy and could tell he was getting a little impatient as well. I spotted him nonchalantly reaching down to his waist band feeling for the pistol. He had it tucked away under his tan jacket where he could get to it in a hurry. Tom had bought the tan jacket at the Antonito train station gift shop. Like me, he was anxious to end this now, but realized there was something more important to do before he could make a move. Controlling his emotions was one of them as he anxiously waited for Mary's instructions.

Mary knew the time was nearing when something was about to happen. She understood from experience that she needed to keep her cool, calm, composure. Hopefully this would prevent Cody and Tom from starting something that could put innocent lives in danger, especially Annie's and JP's. Mary knew the main reason for kidnapping her daughter and grandson was to draw her out of hiding and into the open. What the kidnappers didn't realize is, like a mother grizzly and her cubs, if you steal a mother's children you have just brought the wrath of GOD down on you.

A voice came over the trains speaker system announcing the train was eight miles from the town of Chama, New Mexico. I was standing by the parlor car door pretending to be waiting on an order from one

SEARCH FOR ANNIE

of the passengers, feeling the tension rise. At that moment I spotted Herman Kessler, the youngest of the three kidnappers suddenly jump up and pull the train's emergency stop cord. The sudden stop, created by the activation of the train's emergency braking system, jolted the cars so hard that I was afraid the train cars had jumped the tracks. The loud squealing sound of metal on metal roared loud in our ears. The train passengers that were standing fell over each other and the ones sitting on the Victorian chairs flew off their seats. People started screaming and yelling for help. I had fallen hard against one of the parlor tables, but I hurriedly picked myself up and raced over to my mother-in-law. Mary had been knocked off her seat but showed no sign of injuries. Deputy Kinkaid assisted me in lifting Mary back onto her seat. All three of us looked toward Jim, Annie, and JP. Sudden shock set in as we realized all of them had slipped out the rear door of the parlor car and disappeared.

I raced to the door and stepped outside onto the platform where I spotted the small group of people crossing a two lane highway that ran parallel to the train tracks. Just on the other side of the highway was a small airport. I spotted a DC-3 passenger plane lining up on the runway readying to take off. In an instant I realized what was going to happen. I jumped from the train car platform and ran down the embankment, jumped across a small stream and climbed up the other side bringing me to the edge of the two lane highway. Just as I was about to step out onto the road a loud truck horn broke my concentration. When I was young my mother taught me to look both ways before crossing any roads. I forgot that rule, but quickly remembered it causing me to freeze in place and giving me the scare of my life. I stood there waiting for the impact that could end my life. Fortunately, the truck driver spotted me just in the nick of time and immediately swerved to his left, narrowly missing me by inches. All the passengers on the train were watching as the truck barely missed me. I could feel everyone breathe a sigh of relief, including Mary and Deputy Kinkade who had been watching from the rear platform of the parlor car.

I could hear the plane's twin engines revving up, preparing for takeoff. I raced across the highway and climbed up a small grass covered rise which took me up to the runway behind the plane. I stood there several moments trying to protect myself from the debris blown at me from the backwash of the plane props. The plane started rolling down the runway and I knew I had to do something. I ran with all my strength to catch up to the rear door of the plane. I had the strange idea that I could somehow stop the plane from taking off. The hurricane wind, generated by the propellers back wash, was just too strong for me. I stood there on the runway and watched as the plane took off and climbed into the air then slowly fade out of sight. My heart was crushed, I realized, not only had I lost Annie again, but I lost my son as well. The killing anger I had felt when I realized Annie and JP had been kidnapped started entering my heart again. I now wished I had ignored Mary's advice and just gone ahead and grabbed Annie and JP while they were still on the train. Deep down I still knew Mary was right. We needed to end this three decade long threat; otherwise this would haunt our family the rest of our lives.

I was still standing on the runway watching in the direction the plane had disappeared when Mary came up from behind me and placed her hand on my shoulder.

"I know you probably hate me right now Cody, but if you come with me we'll find out where they are flying to. We will follow them until they get us to the place where they want to end this as bad as we do."

I stood there for a few moments thinking about what she had just said and realized that she had lost just as much as I had.

I answered "I don't hate you mom, I know it wasn't your fault all this happened, but when we get to the place their leading us; I'm going to end this. JP's not going to be raised in this world having to look over his shoulder worrying about the safety of his family. One way or another, this will end with me."

    Mary felt a pinch of happiness when she heard Cody call her mom for the first time since he and Annie had been married. Inside her mind she also knew that she would be the one who would end this evil, even if it took her own life. She knew Cody would take good care of her daughter and grandson and he must never be hurt again because of her failure to end this evil that started several decades earlier.

Chapter VIII

We turned and started to walk to the control tower to join the deputy when a familiar black sedan pulled up to us. Two gentlemen exited the car and approached us. It was Tim Walker and Henry Steel, both of whom are field agents for the CIA and work for Sam Young, the agency's senior commander. I recognized both of them from the last time I saw them more than a year ago. They aided Annie and Jim when they were trying to track me down before I disappeared into the Colorado mountain wilderness.

I said "Well I'll be a monkey's uncle; I never thought I would ever see the two of you again. Mom, I want you to meet two of the men who helped Annie track me down last year. This is Tim Walker and Henry Steel, they work for Sam Young."

Mary instantly knew who they were and thankful that deputy Kinkade was able to get the call through to Sam. She said "Hello gentlemen, I'm happy to see Sam is on top of this."

Henry and Tim greeted Mary with a respectful attitude having heard of her successful exploits during World War II from people in the CIA. They knew of the life threatening situations she had to survive in order to bring back the secret Nazi information she had skillfully collected. The information she had smuggled out was vital to her home country of France and to America. Mary, AKA Maria Annette Marceau, barely escaped Germany with her life and the information she brought out with her was credited for saving thousands of lives.

Henry said "Ma'am, Tim and I were waiting at the train station in Chama, when we heard the train had made an unscheduled stop 8 miles outside town. We figured something was wrong so we raced out here to help, but it looks as if we're a little late."

Mary said "Gentlemen let's go to the control tower and find out where we are to go next."

Tim replied "You say that as if you know what their next move will be."

In a calm collected response Mary answered. "They did all this for one reason, to bring me out of hiding. They want a face to face with the woman who has wanted nothing more, in the last thirty years, than to see me die. Hilda Mueller is behind all this and I guarantee you, she is leaving a trail of clues a mile wide. They want to make sure I don't get lost looking for her." Mary felt a cold chill pass through her body as she

SEARCH FOR ANNIE

softly whispered to herself "Hilda Mueller, I wish I had killed you when I had the chance".

After they had climbed several flights of stairs they entered the small airport's control room. There were two men inside. One man was sitting at a small desk watching a radar screen and calling out instructions to the pilots flying nearby. The other was sitting at a desk in the center of the room studying flight plan requests and listening to the air traffic controller calling out instructions over the radio.

Tim and Henry joined Deputy Kinkade at the airport supervisor's desk where each of them showed their identifications. Tim and Henry started explaining the situation to the airport supervisor while the deputy stepped over to Mary and said "Mrs. Wilson, it looks like this situation is now out of my jurisdiction. I need to head back to my office. I'm anxious to find out how the sheriff is doing and start filling out the paperwork trying to explain everything that has happened so far."

Mary placed her hand on the deputy's forearm and replied "Tom, I understand and I want to thank you for your help. When this is over I hope I will be able to come back and report to you on how this all ended. Take care of yourself and tell the sheriff I'm sorry for all this trouble."

As the deputy disappeared out of the control room Tim and Henry returned to Mary with information.

Henry was the first to speak. "Mrs. Wilson, this is what we know right now according to the supervisor. The plane that took off carrying your family was flown in here two hours earlier with only a pilot and one passenger. The pilot, according to the supervisor, came in here and filed his flight plan. He spoke in English but the supervisor said he had a strong German accent. The pilot also said, to the supervisor that a Mrs. Wilson would be coming here soon and he was to give you this note when you showed up."

Mary took the note from Henry's hand and opened the envelope removing its contents. She unfolded the paper and started reading.

"My Dear Maria,

I wish I could be there with you as you read this. Finally! After all these years of hunting you down I finally get to bring you the pain you have caused me. I have your husband purely by luck but what makes this so sweet is having your daughter and grandson as well. You have no idea how much joy I will get when I have you standing with me, watching the pain I am going to inflict on your daughter. Then after she is dead and just before I kill you I will let you see your grandson die as well. You don't need to thank me for all this because once I am done I'll be able to settle down with my family in our newfound country and enjoy life again. But first, I never let a kind deed go unrewarded. To repay you for being so kind back in 1940, for not plunging that knife into my throat, I am going to give you a chance to save your Grandson. Don't be late; I'll be waiting for you. Just follow the directions below. If I see anyone else, besides you, on the plane when you arrive, I will kill your entire family. SIEGE HEIL !! You're Friend, Hilda Mueller.

Mary's hand was shaking from the anger building inside her. Cody reached over and removed the letter from her hand and started reading the directions. He looked around the room and spotted the navigation charts hanging on the wall behind the supervisor's desk. The map and navigation training he received while in the military was going to pay off again. Mary, Tim, and Henry followed him to the charts and watched as he plotted the coordinates.

They listened as Cody mumbled to himself "Latitude 31degrees 19.0296 minutes' north and longitude 113 degrees 32.2794 minutes west. I turned to Mary and with a deep worried look I said "Mom, their taking my family to a place a few miles east of a Mexican town called Puerto Penasco. It's just sixty miles south of the Arizona border. I've never been there but according to the map it sits right on the northern tip of the Gulf of California."

Tim said "Henry and I will call Sam and let him know where the meeting point is located."

Mary replied "I can't wait for Sam to respond, Cody and I are leaving now."

Henry chimed in and said "But Ma'am how will you get there?"

"Mary answered "There's a Cessna 310 sitting out on the runway. Cody and I will fly it to the meeting place. What Sam and you two gentlemen plan to do is up to you, just don't be late."

Mary met with the airport supervisor for a few minutes and then called for me to follow her. Tim and Henry watched in total amazement as Mary took control of the situation.

When Cody and Mary approached the plane she had rented, Cody asked "When did you learn to fly one of these?"

"Jim taught me 15 years ago for a birthday present; I've just never had a need to fly much. Now I need to. Don't worry, I'm a good pilot. I've only crashed once." she said with a sinister smile.

Tim and Henry watched from the control tower as the plane took off then Henry reached for the phone and dialed Washington.

Chapter IX

Back at CIA headquarters in Washington, D.C., Sam was sitting at his large maple wood desk shuffling through a stack of papers. He vaguely remembered an operative's report that came in from Panama a month earlier that said a suspicious yacht had just passed through the canal sailing west to the Pacific. Sam, who has been with the CIA, before its conception in 1947, was now in his early sixties. He had been receiving a lot of political suggestions that it might be wise to step down and hand the reins over to the younger generation. While all his friends and mentors succumbed to the pressures by their peers and retired, Sam decided he wasn't going to give up so easily. Trying hard to fight back and prove that he was more than capable of doing his job, he was bound and determined to capture these Nazi agents and bring them to justice. He felt this would prove, once and for all, he could still handle the job.

The pager on his phone came alive with Melissa's

voice saying "Sir! I have Henry on line one."

Sam punched the button for line one and with his deep baritone voice, said "Sam here! Henry, what's going on out there?"

Henry explained the current situation, "Tim and I arrived too late to help stop the flight that took Jim, Anne, and JP south to Mexico. According to the letter, Hilda had left behind for Mary; she is to fly to a designated spot in Mexico to get her family back. Cody plotted the course that pinpointed a small landing strip in Mexico just east of a village called Puerto Penasco."

Next came a surprise that Sam wasn't expecting. Henry said "Sir, Mary has rented a four seat Cessna that was being kept here at the airport. She is flying Cody and herself to Mexico. She wanted to know if Tim and I were coming with her, if so, we'll be leaving in fifteen minutes."

Sam replied, in a loud voice that even Melissa could hear as she sat at her desk outside his closed office door. "WHAT? WHEN DID SHE LEARN HOW TO FLY? She can't do this without back up! Let me talk to her!!"

Henry replied "Sir, she said there is no time for talk and she will see you, GOD willing, in Mexico."

Sam replied loudly "YOU AND TIM WAIT THERE, I've got another plan." Sam slammed the phone down grumbling under his breath as he punched the pager button "Melissa! Get me Captain Armstrong over at our military training base in Quantico! Also have our jet ready to take off immediately."

Melissa was a slender, brown eyed, 5foot 8 inch brunette. She has been working with Sam for nearly twenty years now and knows from experience how to temper his anxieties; including, keeping his blood pressure from exploding. She walked into his office and could see his increase of tension begin to calm down. She was nearly forty now and knew working with Sam would soon be over. She understood the pressures he was under to retire and how they were beginning to take their toll on him. She realized that one day it would finally happen and felt no more ready for the change than he did.

Eventually time will catch up with you whether you want it to or not. It doesn't matter if it's a husband and wife providing for and raising their children, or if it is a professional person who dedicates their life to a chosen career. It has always been and always will be difficult for each person to accept the fact that they have gotten older. Their age and physical condition will no longer allow them to achieve the goals they had set for themselves. When we have reached that point in our life, we can only pray that our physical and mental abilities will still allow us a useful place in life to finish out our remaining years. The hope is that, we will be able to help the next generation learn from our successes and failures.

After all these years with Sam, Melissa could almost read his thoughts as she said "Sir, I have Michael from research on line one and the company plane on standby."

Sam looked up from his desk and smiled at her "Melissa, I don't know what I'd do without you."

She smiled and said "Sir, you wouldn't be able to get along without me and the paper you're looking for is the twelfth one down in the stack of papers on your left."

He reached over to the left hand stack of papers on his desk and pulled out the twelfth page. He looked up in amazement as Melissa smiled and closed the door.

Sam picked up his phone and punched line one saying. "Mike, I need all the info I can get on Puerto Penasco, Mexico. Have Buddy dig up all the information he can on a yacht that sailed through the Panama Canal about three weeks ago with the name HILDA written on its stern. I need it all by yesterday. Also, let me know who our contacts are in that region."

Sam punched the pager button for Melissa who had anticipated Sam's next move and on hearing his page she said "Sir, I have London on line two."

Sam smiled and replied "Thanks Melissa."

Chapter X

It was nearly 4pm when Mary leveled off the twin engine Cessna-310 as she navigated the flight plan instructions Hilda had left for her. Mary flew south at a low altitude to avoid any radar detection that might create border trouble from the American or Mexican authorities.

She looked over at Cody who was sitting in the co-pilot's seat and said "When we reach our destination it will be dark. Once we get there, you stay low and out of sight. After I land the plane I will fly it to the end of the runway and make a 180 degree turn leaving it ready for takeoff again. After I exit the plane, you wait ten minutes, and then exit the passenger door on the blind side of the plane. After you exit, duck into the shadows where you'll be able to hide until you can carefully work yourself into a position to see and hear what's going on. Whoever is there waiting will be waiting for and watching me. It should be dark enough for you to slip out the blind side of the plane without being seen. Don't try anything until I have their attention entirely on me! OK?"

I replied "Yes Ma'am." I was impressed with her strong ability to express her plans in clear and precise language to me and still be able to fly low, weaving in and out, between the desert hills. I began to feel as if I were back in Vietnam again flying in a chopper at treetop level. My combat training and experience were coming back to me as I told myself *'The enemy is different but the killing would be the same.'*

I watched the desert floor race by and noticed the long shadows of the tall saguaros. I must have been feeling really tired because as we flew south over the Saguaros their shadows appeared to look like crosses warning us of danger just ahead. I looked off towards the west at the setting sun. I was reminded of the time I first saw Annie three years earlier. It was when I boarded the plane that was flying me and other young soldiers to Vietnam. There, sitting on board, was Annie. I felt the ache in my heart return for not being at home this morning to save her and JP from these kidnappers. I also felt my anger return for the trouble these people have caused us and knew that, one way or another, this trouble would soon end.

At that same moment in another plane flying several miles ahead Annie was wishing this day had never

SEARCH FOR ANNIE

started. She was still holding JP in her lap looking west out of her small plane window watching the sun set behind the desert mountains. She worried about Cody and her mother, hoping they were alright, and close behind. She tried not to show any sign of worry but her father, sitting beside her, could see the concern on Annie's face. He reached over and placed his hand on hers.

When she looked up at him, he smiled and said in a soft voice "Don't worry sweetheart everything will be alright."

Just then the pilot began talking, in German, to someone on the radio. He then began a slow bank left and the plane began to descend in altitude. Annie could see forward enough to make out a small airfield with its landing lights on. The plane gently glided down until its wheels landed smoothly on the sandy runway. Annie watched out her window as the plane rolled past what looked like a large airport hangar and a long building that reminded her of a basic training barracks. She had spent some time in one while going through Army nursing school. She also spotted a shorter building next to it that could be a control room.

Jim, who was watching out the same window suddenly, felt a cold chill. He noticed the buildings seem to be laid out in the same configuration as the airport buildings he, Paul Miller, and Maria escaped, from thirty years ago. They escaped by flying out in a stolen Nazi patrol plane. Jim remembered racing down the runway for take off and seeing Hilda with Gestapo agent Major Kessler standing just outside the airport's control room. Major Kessler was shooting at them with his 9mm Lugar as they raced by for takeoff. Jim did recognize one difference about this air base compared with the one in Germany and that was the lack of tall trees around its perimeter.

The plane taxied its way off the main runway and stopped in front of the barracks looking building. Herman Kessler exited first after lowering the fold out steps for the others who followed. They all stood just outside the plane in the dim evening twilight. Annie, holding tight to JP, could feel her father get closer to her. She looked up at the darkening sky and noticed several stars had appeared. Two bright flood lights snapped on and lit up the area around the plane. JP was getting restless and wanted to eat.

Just then the door to the barracks opened and two dark figures stepped out into the light. One appeared to be an old man in his late sixties or early seventies who walked with the use of a cane. He wore an old black German trench coat wrapped loosely around his shoulders. Covering his head was a black fedora hat, whose rim was pulled down to where it rested a few centimeters above his bushy white eyebrows. The trench coat ran all the way down to his ankles. The old man's wrinkled and scarred face seemed familiar to Jim.

Jim was trying to remember where he had seen the old man when he looked at the woman holding on to the old man's arm. Immediately he recognized her.

"Hilda Mueller", he whispered. She looked older, but she still had her evil appearance. She was wearing a light brown skirt and shirt that reminded him of the Nazi youth uniforms from the thirties. He noticed the German swastika pins on the collar of her shirt. Slowly, and with caution, Jim carefully stepped in front of Annie and JP.

Hilda let go of the old man's arm, stomped right up to Jim, and stood only a few inches away from his face. Her cold blue eyes glared straight into his calm brown eyes. With a cruel mean tone in her voice she said "I told you that one day I would find you and Maria again! Now, all we have to do is wait for Maria to land and it will be like old times. Only this time, instead of her holding the knife to my throat, I'll be the one holding the knife to her throat." She gave Jim an evil grin and then turned toward her husband, Adolf Kessler. Wrapping her arms around his left arm she leaned over to him and gave Adolf a kiss on the cheek and said, "Sweetheart, you and our sons have done me and the fatherland proud. You also bring pride to our father Major Kessler!"

When Jim heard the name, he was stunned. He thought, *'after all these years I assumed he would have been dead.'* When Hilda said his name Jim immediately recognized him and said "Well Major Kessler, I thought you would have been dead by now. Several agencies around the world in different countries have been searching for you. Where have you been hiding?"

The old man came up close to Jim and stared at him for several seconds before he said in a crusty old voice "Herr Wilson, like you, I have been hiding in plain sight." The Major stared past Jim at Annie and her baby. Annie could feel the fear run down her spine as the Major slowly approached her. She could see several scars on his old wrinkled face and feel the hateful evil pouring out from his eyes. Jim stepped back to block his approach to Annie. Hilda's eldest son, Martin, who stood 2 inches taller than Jim and outweighed him by a good fifty pounds, stepped over to Jim. He grabbed Jim's collar and yanked him out of the way. Jim could feel his blood come to a boil but he knew he couldn't do anything yet without putting Annie and the baby into more danger.

The old man looked Annie over and then looked at the baby. "With these two as our bait I guarantee Maria will be here soon!"

Herman, Hilda's youngest son was feeling a bit irritated with all the greetings and niceties going on and

SEARCH FOR ANNIE

interjected "Why not just kill them now and get it over with? You know Maria will be along soon and when she gets here we'll have completed part of our mission."

Hilda replied in an angry voice "Because, you dummkopf, if she doesn't see them alive she won't land. Now keep your stupid ideas to yourself and take the three of them to the storage room, inside the barracks building, and lock them in until we need them!"

Jim was surprised when he heard Herman say 'part of our mission'. He could see the evil glare Hilda gave him for revealing more information than what he should have. The embarrassment Herman was feeling for allowing his young impatience to get out of control gave Jim an idea. He needed to get this young man in a one on one situation. He felt if he could get him alone he might be able to get him to reveal more information. He needed to find out about the other part of their mission. Herman, holding a 9mm Lugar, escorted Jim, Annie, and JP into the barracks building where he directed them into a backroom. The room was roughly twenty feet wide and ten feet deep. It was lit up by only one dim forty watt lightbulb dangling at the end of a single wire from the 8ft tall ceiling. Other than two chairs the room was void of any other furniture and had no windows.

Jim, using his soft fatherly voice said to Herman "She was rough on you out there wasn't she?"

Herman replied in a stern voice "My mother has always been strict with me. Sometimes I deserve it. I know the difficult life she has been through. I also know she doesn't want Martin and me to need for anything. She told us how you, Herr Miller, with Maria, had destroyed her life, killed her father, and ruined the Nazi party. Our Grandfather Kessler was able to get permission from our party supreme leader, Herr Adolf Hitler, to capture and eliminate you before we continue with our primary mission."

The name, Jim had just heard the young man mention, sent a cold chill through him as he replied "You say Adolf Hitler as if he was still alive."

Herman grinned and replied "Despite what the world thinks, our supreme leader lives on."

Before Herman closed the door, Jim said "That primary mission you mentioned must be important, why not do it first before you kill us?"

Herman answered "Because mother wants to do it at the same time we kill all of you. She says it will be a day when all Nazi party members will celebrate their triumphant return to power. She has a great vision of, one day, becoming its leader."

Jim then asked "What is this primary mission that makes it so special?"

Herman turned from the door, looked straight at Jim and said "Killing your President."

Chapter XI

Young Herman, with an irritating grin on his face, exited the small windowless room with its single 40 watt lightbulb and locked the door behind him. Jim started pacing the room trying to think of a way to end this terror before Mary flew in. Anne was sitting on one of the two chairs cradling JP in her arms humming the tune 'Hush Little Baby Don't You Cry'. At the same time she worried about Cody and wondered where he might be. Jim's anxiety was boiling over as he tried to understand the chilling news he had just heard. He was still wearing the train conductor's uniform he had acquired at the Antonito train station back in Colorado. He paid the train conductor fifty bucks for the uniform, only to have it end up being a failed disguise. Right now though, he stood in the middle of the small room in deep thought, thinking about what young Herman had just told him. *'If their number one reason for this whole scenario was to kill our president how were they going to do it from here?'*

Annie had been quiet through most of this ordeal. She was sitting on one of the two chairs feeding JP. He was eating a container of baby food she had managed to hurriedly stuff into the diaper bag, along with, five filled baby bottles and several diapers. It was all she had time to gather up before the kidnappers rushed her and JP out of their house into the back of a black van and raced away.

Holding JP she looked up at her father and asked "Dad, how are we going to stop these people from killing the President? I thought we were their primary mission!"

Jim turned toward Annie and sat down on the chair beside her. He looked into her lovely blue eyes and said "I'm not sure sweetheart apparently we're just the sideshow for Hilda. The main event will take place after she eliminates us. Right now she is waiting for your mother to show up, and then the game will begin."

Jim leaned closer to Annie and whispered softly in her ear, "There's a listening device planted on the light hanging from the ceiling so be careful about what you say out loud. I'm hoping the deputy got my message to Sam. If he did we can expect the action around here to pick up. I only wish I knew what your mother and Cody were getting ready to do."

SEARCH FOR ANNIE

A few miles away, flying the twin engine Cessna, Mary's voice crackled over the radio headsets she and Cody were wearing. "Cody! Inside my purse you'll find a Smith and Wesson 32, it's only a cylinder six shot, so make each one count. Get it and keep it with you. I need you to lie down on the floor between the two seats in back. We're getting close to our destination and we can't afford any mistakes. Just as a reminder, when I land I'm going to run the plane to the end of the runway. Then I'm going to spin it around and get it ready for takeoff. Once I exit the plane you wait a few minutes, then you exit the side of the plane away from their view. Work your way around to a point where you can see and hear everything going on. When trouble begins I want you to be able to rush in and get Anne and JP out. We're playing this by ear so if anything goes wrong your main mission is to get Annie and JP out alive. Jim and I will do what we can to eliminate the danger and protect your escape."

"Don't worry mom, I've had plenty of experience at covert operations. When the right time comes you can count on me to get Annie and JP out safely."

Mary felt a twinge of happiness when Cody called her mom. She also felt his past military experience would be what could make the difference in getting them out alive. She reached over and squeezed his hand letting him know she had the utmost confidence in him.

Hilda, Adolf, and Hermann Kessler were in the control building sitting around the table with Hilda's father-in-law, Major Kessler, when Martin came rushing through the door saying "The plane is coming!"

All of them hurried out the door into the dark night. Hilda hollered for Martin to turn on the runway lights, whose switch was on the control building wall next to the exit door. She and the rest of the group walked over to the barracks building. She ordered Herman to get the prisoners and bring them out. Adding to this crisis came five well-armed gunmen, hired by Hilda, racing out of the control building to join them. Jim noticed the tall antenna on the control building and figured there was a radio transmitter inside. Herman returned to the group, escorting Annie, Jim, and JP at gunpoint. He pushed the trio to the front of the crowd where they stood with everyone else watching the lights of the twin engine Cessna approach.

Mary yelled at me above the noise of the twin engines, "They just switched on the runway lights; we're going in for the landing. I can see a large group of people standing near the runway and the plane they took off in is parked nearby."

I was lying on the airplane floor, hidden from sight

behind the two rear seats when I heard Mary's voice say "We'll be touching down in 5, 4,3,2,1... Touch down. I felt the hard thump as the wheels touched down and heard the props go in reverse to help slow our speed.

Mary continued to say "I can see one large hangar, one long building that looks like a barracks and a third building that looks like it could be a control room.

When she described the set up to Cody a chill came over her as she remembered the same set up of buildings, thirty years earlier, where she had held a knife to Hilda's throat.

Mary brought the twin engine Cessna in, landing it as smoothly as she could on the sandy desert runway. When she sped by the group of people standing at the runways edge she could easily see Jim, Annie, and JP, who were surrounded by ten other people. When she reached the end of the runway she revved up the engines and pushed the right brake pedal down hard causing the plane to spin around so that it would be ready to take off again.

Annie whispered to her father "Looks like those flying lessons you gave mom really paid off."

While she shut off the engines and unbuckled her seat belt she quietly spoke, only loud enough for Cody to hear. "There are ten other people standing around our three family members. Three of them, I remember seeing on the train. The female has to be Hilda, the old man I don't recognize but the other five young men are muscle and undoubtedly heavily armed, so be careful and good luck."

At that point Mary pushed the pilot's hatch door open and stepped out onto the wing where she stood for a few moments starring straight at Hilda. She was determined not to show fear and had already devised a plan that would help Cody exit the plane without being seen. She knew she had to get everyone's attention away from the plane to give Cody a chance to exit. When she joined the awaiting group she immediately wrapped her arms around Annie and JP giving them a hug. Taking JP from Annie's arms she stepped to the other side of the group, to a more lighted area created by the outdoor light on the barracks building. She could see everyone's eyes were on her. Jim's feelings began to feel hurt when Mary didn't hug or kiss him or even acknowledge his existence. But when he saw everyone turn their backs to the plane to keep an eye on Mary, he knew she had made the move to cover someone exiting the plane. Jim had a strong feeling he knew who it would be.

***

When I heard Mary step off the plane I crawled out from my hiding place behind the two rear seats. Staying low and out of sight I carefully and quietly, crawled forward to the co-pilots position. Lifting my head up over the instrument panel just far enough to peek out the window, I watched as Mary reached the waiting group at the edge of the landing field. When I saw her take JP from Annie's arms I noticed how smoothly Mary stepped to the other side of the group, causing them to turn their backs to the plane. I knew she did it on purpose giving me the opportunity to slip out the co-pilots darkened side of the plane.

My experiences from the months of night patrols in Vietnam were flooding back into my memory. The knowledge I had learned from each patrol was paying off again. Knowing that, at night, sound carries farther than it does during the day made me more cautious. I slowly and carefully opened the passenger door located behind the co-pilots seat. Warily I began to gently open the door just far enough to allow me to slither out onto the wing. Vigilantly I dropped off the wing to the ground where I flattened out and stayed motionless for a few moments listening for any hint that I may have been spotted. Hearing only the faint mumbling of the group over by Mary, I crawled on my belly past the tail of the plane and slipped behind a small sand dune.

I used the cover of the sand dune and the many desert cacti to cover my movements. Using the light from the half moon, I worked my way to the back left corner of, what I believe, was the barracks building.

RON MAHAFFEY

I figured if anyone would spot me it would be Mary, who was cunning and sharp enough to spot any movement near or far.

I laid on the ground at the back corner of what Mary described to me to be a barracks building. I cautiously, crawled along the side of the building until I reached its front corner. Staying low to the ground I carefully peeked around the corner toward the group out front. I was now close enough that I could hear their conversations. Some of it was spoken in German, but Mary, knowing I was listening, skillfully kept guiding the conversation back to English.

Chapter XII

Hilda's patience was wearing thin. Several minutes passed by as she tried to verbally intimidate Maria with fear, threats, and bodily harm. She had hoped Maria would be begging her for mercy by now, but Maria only ignored her. Hilda was outraged by Maria's total lack of awareness and no sign of fear. This made Hilda's thirst for Maria's blood go ballistic. Hilda charged toward Maria and tried to snatch JP from her arms, but Maria moved quickly and slapped Hilda's arm away.

Hilda felt shock and anger as the embarrassment of what Maria had just done created a few chuckles from the on lookers. She said in a wicked, vile, tone "If it was up to me, I would kill you and your entire family right now; starting with that little brat grandson of yours, then your ugly daughter and stupid husband. I plan on saving you for last so I can watch you suffer through each kill."

Maria, seeing how much she had irritated Hilda

replied. "Are you going to do it yourself or are you still the little coward you've always been and let someone else do your dirty work for you?"

Hilda started forward again to strike Maria, but the elderly gentlemen holding himself up with a cane grabbed Hilda by the arm stopping her. Maria hadn't recognized him yet until he said "Not so fast Hilda darling, we have our other business to complete first, than you may begin your fun." Mary instantly recognized the man's voice, opening the floodgate to some difficult memories from years ago. Memories of a beating she received from Gestapo Agent, Major Kessler, back in Germany, in early spring of nineteen forty.

Mary handed JP back to Annie and turned toward the old man saying, with a questionable tone in her voice "I know you, don't I? You must be the Gestapo agent that enjoys beating up little girls. It's a pity the war didn't kill you Major Kessler."

Kessler smiled and said "Sehr gute Frau Wilson, I was hoping you would remember the beating I gave you during our last encounter because this time there will be no one to save you."

Maria remembered, all too well, the beating he had given her, back in 1940, just minutes before Jim and Paul Allen had rescued her. Suddenly Mary's memory flashed and she remembered that it wasn't Jim and Paul who saved her life that night it was Nazi

SEARCH FOR ANNIE

General Muller, Hilda's father. He had knocked out Major Kessler and untied Maria before Jim and Paul showed up. It was at that time when Hilda's father told them that he was actually a British agent. He told them he had infiltrated deep within the Nazi regime and was gathering information to send home, to MI-6, on Hitler's plan to invade France. Mary felt no fear of Major Kessler anymore and knew with Cody nearby, Annie and JP would be safe. She wondered whether Hilda had ever learned about her father's true identity, but decided she would wait until the right moment to ask her. Right now, Maria was worried about what Kessler meant when he stopped Hilda and said, 'We have other business to complete first.'

Hilda knew Kessler was right; she could wait just a little longer before she completed her lifelong hunt for revenge. She turned toward the five hired gunman and in her loud commanding voice, ordered the five mercenaries, "TAKE THEM ALL AND LOCK THEM UP IN THE STORAGE ROOM OF THE BARRACKS!"

I watched and listened to the entire event from my hiding place at the dark corner of the barracks building. When the five guards escorted my family into the barracks building, I slowly slipped back along the side of it until I was out of sight. Then, trying to be silent as a cat, I slowly lifted myself up off the sandy ground and slipped noiselessly the rest of the way to the rear of the building. Carefully, I peered around its corner and spotted two windows where light from within was flowing out reflecting off the beige colored sandy desert floor, creating an eerie ghostly glow. Before moving any farther, I methodically scanned the area for any signs of a security guard. Spotting no unusual movements and not hearing any unusual noise I warily approached the first window. I guardedly peeked through its lower right corner, watching the five gunmen as they ushered Annie and her family into a room then closing and locking its door. I ducked down out of site and listened to one of the gunmen, speaking German, give orders to another gunman. I understood some of the language and interpreted two of the words, 'stay here'. I watched the other four hired killers walk out of the barracks and follow Hilda and the rest of her group into the large hangar building and close the door behind them.

I pulled out the six shot snub nose 32, Mary had given to me just before she landed the plane. I knew it wasn't going to be enough fire power to fight them all off but, I could surprise and disarm the one guarding the locked door. That would give me access to his Thompson 45caliber submachine gun. Capturing that gun would increase our odds of survival. Thanks to Uncle Sam, I had used one during my tour in Nam and confidently understood its mechanical operation.

SEARCH FOR ANNIE

I had to act quickly, before Hilda and her entourage returned from the hangar. I hesitated for a moment while my mind tried to decide on what my next move should be. My little voice kept, hauntingly, asking me over and over "What was in that hangar that drew Hilda and her band of thugs away from, what I had always thought was, their primary objective. According to Mary, she and her family had always been Hilda's main objective. I wonder what change had transpired to alter Hilda's lifelong quest".

I pushed those thoughts to the back of my mind as I cautiously crept around to the front of the barracks building. Silently, I reached its door and unscrewed the light bold which covered me with darkness. Using the experience I had learned while watching my two cats trying to trick their way into my house, I scratched the door of the barracks with my fingernails and followed up with a truly accurate "meow". I performed this imitation two more times before I heard the guard's footsteps inside, slowly approach the door. I silently pressed myself back against the barracks wall next to the door waiting nervously, for it to open.

I heard the door handle turn and watched it start to open. I knew if I failed to quietly subdue the guard our hope of escaping would be lost. My entire family, along with me, would only be one bullet away from termination. The door opened and the guard stepped forward

RON MAHAFFEY

to find that mangy old cat. I quickly pointed my 32 into the guards face and pulled the hammer back saying, "HANDS UP!"

I couldn't believe what I saw when I pushed the guard back into the barracks. To my surprise, the guard had left his machine gun hanging by its sling on the back of the chair he had been sitting on. I looked at the guard, whose look of fear was slowly turning into anger, and said to him "careful comrade, one false move and I will kill you!" I used broken English and some hand signaling to order the guard to lay face down on the floor with his hands behind his head.

I stepped over to his spread out body lying on the floor and carefully removed the keys from his pocket. I searched him for any hidden weapons and finding none, I quickly grabbed the machine gun from the back of the chair and slung it over my shoulder. While still keeping an eye on my prisoner I unlocked and opened the door to the back room where Annie, JP, and her family were being kept.

Jim, having heard the sounds of footsteps and mumbling of voices coming from outside their room, assumed the guards were coming back to execute his family. Jim wasn't going to give up without a fight. When he heard the door to their room begin to open

SEARCH FOR ANNIE

he jumped to one side of it. He hoped he could grab the first guard and take his weapon away. While waiting for the guard to enter he watched Annie's face for an indication of who was entering the room. He watched, with nerves on edge, as Annie's face went from fear to joy. She instantly handed JP to her mother and quickly jumped up from the wooden chair and ran to Cody. Tightly wrapping her arms around his neck she kissed him hard on the lips. Jim stepped out from behind the door and spotted the guard lying on the floor. He was slowly moving his hands into a position where he could spring up and escape or attack.

Jim grabbed the Smith and Wesson32 from Cody's hand and pointed it at the guards head whispering, so no one listening over the bug could hear, "I wouldn't do that unless you have a death wish!"

Mary, who had been holding JP in her arms, quickly got up and handed JP to Anne whispering. "You and Cody take JP and get out of here. Your father and I are going to finish this."

Jim reached up and disabled the listening devise and handed Mary the 32 Smith and Wesson. Who then, showing her years of experience dealing with guns, skillfully checked the pistol and its unfired rounds. She quickly stepped over to the door and slowly turned the knob. She carefully opened it just far enough to peek out around its edge. Mary looked for any sign of Hilda or her group returning from the hangar. Jim found a small roll of wire that was left lying on the floor, probably left there by the electricians who built this place. Jim and I tied up and gagged the guard, then dragged his heavy body into the backroom and closed the door. Now that we had him securely put away the rest of us quietly slipped out the door. We moved cautiously along the dimly lit exterior front edge of the weather worn wood siding wall. A shadow on the front of the building, created by the roof overhang, gave us some cover. Jim led the way as we slowly slipped across the front of the building and around the corner. When everyone had turned the corner out of sight, Jim took a moment for one last look around. He just wanted to make sure we hadn't been spotted. He led our small group to an area behind the plane Mary and I had landed. We proceeded to a sand dune that would hide us from site.

Mary started to ask me to take Annie and JP out on the plane while she and Jim covered our escape. I had already anticipated her statement and replied in a low whisper "You take Annie and JP out while dad and I cover your take off. I can't fly a twin engine and you can. Once you get airborne use the radio and call Sam. Tell him where we are and get us help ASAP!"

Just as Mary, Annie, and JP were preparing to leave our hiding spot to board the plane, there was a gunshot

SEARCH FOR ANNIE

and a loud yell coming from the direction of the barracks building. Instantly the door to the hangar popped open and Hilda ran out shouting "WHO ESCAPED?"

The guard who found them missing ran up to Hilda saying "They are all gone!"

Hilda's face went blood red with anger. She grabbed a pistol from the security guard nearest her and stomped over to the barracks building. When she entered, she stormed over to the security guard who had been watching the prisoners. He had just been untied from his bindings and was beginning to stand up. A few moments later a gunshot was heard. Hilda walked out of the building with a smoking pistol barrel and a small grin on her face.

"Herr Ralph will never make that mistake again." She stated with a slight chuckle.

She then turned to the rest of her group and said in a loud voice "THE REST OF YOU SPREAD OUT AND FIND THEM! It will be daylight soon and we need to complete our mission and get out of here".

Jim turned to Cody "Take the women and my grandson away from here. Stay down low behind the sand dune and follow it east over to that arroyo. Get them as far away from here as quickly as you can. I'm going to try and get them to follow me the other direction and hopefully lead them away from you. Once I feel you're in the clear I'm going to lose them and circle back. I need to find out what's in that hangar."

Mary, having overheard what Jim had just said, stated "You aren't going to do this alone! We've been a team for over thirty years now and I'll be damned if I'm going to lose you now, not after all we've been through!"

Jim looked at Mary and knew there was no way he'd be able to change her mind. Even in the moonlight he could still see her determination in those beautiful blue eyes, the same color blue that Annie had inherited. It reminded him of the first time he looked into them. It was back in 1940, while in the back of the 1937 Peugeut 402, behind German lines. They were racing only minutes ahead of the Nazi SS who were hunting for her because they had discovered she was a French spy. If they were captured it meant only one thing, torture and an excruciating slow death...

Now here they were again, over thirty years later, trying to escape the same Nazi criminals. Only this time it involved the whole family.

Jim looked tenderly at Mary and said "Ok sweetheart, lets end this together!"

Mary turned to Cody and said, "I need you to take Annie and JP out of here. There's a small town about seven miles to the east. You can see its lights shining low in the eastern horizon. The sun will be up in three more hours. You will need to be as far away from here as you can get. It will keep you from being spotted in this open desert country. Once you arrive try to contact Sam, tell him where we are and ask him to send help ASAP. Tell him we believe there is a terrorist threat against the U.S."

I replied "Yes ma'am, you will need this, take this machine gun I took off the security guard and give me the 32. You'll need more firepower than I will. Good luck to the both of you."

Knowing their odds of coming out of this alive I timidly added "We'll see you later."

When I said that, a cold feeling came over me. I hadn't felt it since the last time I saw my friends who had been killed in the rocket attack the night I proposed to Annie. I began to wonder what had happened to Tom, Sam, and JJ, the only three out of the six of us that survived. I quickly shook the thoughts off and concentrated on getting JP and Annie out of here to safety.

Annie, holding JP, looked into her mother and fathers eyes. She knew there was nothing more she could do or say as tears slowly slipped down her cheek. She gave each of them a loving hug and a kiss, and then forced a smile for them before she turned back to me. I tucked the 32 into the back of my pants behind my belt. I then reached over to Annie and took the diaper bag, with JP's last bottle inside, off her shoulder. I tossed the strap over my shoulder and took Annie by the hand. We pushed off east into the moon lit desert staying under cover behind the desert vegetation and following the arroyos until we were clear of the airport. We had only the moonlight to show us the way. The distant man made city lights glowing on the low horizon help to guide us. We slowly and cautiously disappeared into the cactus filled, dry, sandy desert.

Jim and Mary watched Cody and Annie disappear into the bright moon lit desert, and then turned their focus on Hilda and her entourage. Hilda was shouting out orders to her mercenaries just as if she had been trained by her father. Her father happened to be General Muller of the Nazi Second Panzer Division. He was reported missing on the Russian front in nineteen forty two. He probably would have been proud of her if it wasn't for the fact he was actually a British agent with MI-6. He was able to infiltrate the Nazi party in nineteen thirty one.

Jim could hear Hilda shouting her orders as she ordered Herman to go check the airplane. Jim leaned toward Mary and whispered "It's time for us to move."

Annie and I hadn't gone very far when JP started to cry. I quickly reached into the diaper bag and retrieved the last bottle of formula handing it to Annie.

SEARCH FOR ANNIE

She carefully laid JP down on the sandy desert floor and skillfully changed his diaper while JP contentedly drank his brew. I was impressed with her speed in which she performed the thankless task. There's no way in the world I could have done that task any better. It seemed like only a few minutes and we were all up and traveling again.

Chapter XIII

Herman Goring Kessler, the youngest son of Hilda Muller Kessler, had just finished checking the inside of the twin engine, six passengers Cessna, as his mother had ordered him to do. When, just as he stepped off the wing onto the ground, he heard what he thought sounded like a baby cry. Herman had spent a few years, of his twenty years of young life, living in mostly secluded, remote areas. They always seemed to be on the run, hunted by nearly every country in the world. During his stays in these isolated spots he had ample opportunity to study and learn a lot about tracking the wildlife. That's where he learned their different habits and sounds. He knew that a cougar, when it growls, makes a sound that is similar to that of a crying baby. He was also aware the escaped prisoners they were looking for had a baby whose mother was a very good looking woman.

Herman, like most young men, had an active imagination. He started thinking about their trip down here and started imagining seeing Annie looking at him in an admiring way. He felt he was the better looking of the family and she was attracted to him. For some strange reason, he felt deep in his heart, she had given him signs that she had affections for him. With that in mind he knew he had to find her and take her away with him.

He thought for a few minutes and decided that if he could capture the woman and baby, plus kill Frau Maria and her husband his mother would show him respect. She would probably let him keep the good looking woman for himself. It also dawned on him that by saving the woman and her child then possibly, the woman herself would be grateful to him and possibly think of him as her hero. Herman's pride swelled with his newly found grand idea.

Herman stared off into the desert. He figured the mother and baby would head east toward the distant city lights. He checked his weapon and ammunition and then picked up a canteen of water and headed out in the direction in which he heard the baby cry. He felt the excitement inside himself grow, giving him the feeling of being a big game hunter, hunting a wild animal for his trophy case. Only in this case, his prize would be a beautiful blue eyed woman called Annie and his only kill would be the people his mother wanted dead. He had to hurry, time was running out.

It has been a few years since Mary and Jim had used their special ops training, courtesy of the CIA. Jim and Mary, using the cover of the local cacti, sand dunes, and moonlight, were able to move quietly and cautiously along the eastern side of the airport runway. Staying out of sight they safely moved the length of the runway crawling the last few feet to an area that had sufficient vegetation for cover. They lay there, resting while trying to come up with a plan that would give them access to the hangar.

Mary kept an eye on their back trail, making sure no one had spotted them. Because of the bright moonlight they were able to see Herman as he climbed onto the airplane's wing and enter the plane's passenger door. Jim motioned to Mary to follow him as he moved further up the east side of the runway. They reached an area directly across from the airports hangar building that Hilda and Kessler had entered earlier that evening.

They were able to move from one spot to another with the help of the shadows created by the moonlight and the desert vegetation. The empty shipping crates strung out along the length of the runway were ideal hiding places. Using them made moving further up the runway easier. They went from one crate to another until they reached a point directly across from the northern end of the hangar building. The only problem they faced now was the fifty yards of open ground they had to cover to cross the runway before they reached a hiding place beside the dark hangar. The bright moonlight made it almost impossible to cross the open ground without being spotted. Mary laid there on the sandy desert floor and rested a few minutes while Jim tried to come up with a plan to get across the open ground without being seen. She stared up at the stars finding the Big Dipper and Orion's belt. She marveled at the beauty the moonlight created reflecting its light off the approaching clouds giving them a silvery edge and casting a dark shadow over the ground as they floated silent and free toward them.

Jim was scanning the surrounding area for another way to approach the hangar when Mary nudged him.

He looked at her as she pointed up to the dark sky and the stars. At first he thought she just wanted to show him the beauty of it all, but when he just shrugged his shoulders and looked away she pinched him on the bottom. He started to feel annoyance stir inside himself until he looked at her again and could see in her face a stern look that told him she had spotted something.

He turned and looked in the direction she had pointed and saw what she was trying, so desperately, to indicate to him. Clouds were moving in that would soon block the moonlight. They would then be able to cross the open ground quickly giving them a very slim chance of being spotted.

Jim and Mary watched as the cloud moved across the face of the moon throwing the entire area into darkness, covering it like a dark blanket. Like cats they leaped up and raced across the open area to the hangar where they ducked out of sight behind some wooden crates. Both of them breathed heavily from the run. Jim, panting heavily, whispered "I think we made it without being seen, but I don't think I'm as young as I use to be."

Mary, who was still breathing heavily herself smiled as she replied "Sweetheart, I don't believe either of us are that young anymore."

After several minutes of scanning the area and listening for any unusual sounds, Jim and Mary decided it was time to move. They looked out from behind their cover of empty wooden crates and searched for their next possible hiding place. Jim's curiosity kept asking him *'Why? With the limited size of aircraft that could land here, was the hangar so large?'* The size only added more fuel to his curiosity to find out its contents. The clouds had drifted away and the moonlight was creating spooky shadows on everything that was exposed to its light. Mary spotted, what appeared to be, a dark square shaped hole in the side of the hangar about twenty five feet away. She tapped Jim on the shoulder and pointed to it. He nodded his head in understanding

SEARCH FOR ANNIE

and motioned for Mary to follow him. They cautiously moved out from behind the crates and like quiet cats, they moved carefully to the darkened spot.

When they arrived they discovered the dark looking patch on the side of the hangar was a square, four by four foot open air vent that appeared to lead inside the hangar. They could see light seeping through the slots of the air vent cover about ten feet inside. Without saying a word they looked at each other and Jim signaled to Mary to crawl inside. Mary entered first while Jim scanned the area one last time then followed Mary in.

Mary reached the end of the air vent and started peering through the slots quickly scanning the insides of the hangar as Jim slid up beside her.

"See anything unusual?" he quietly whispered.

"There is a huge tarp covering something that's nearly the same length as the hangar." Mary whispered.

Jim looked through one of the vent slots and could see what Mary had described. He also could hear voices inside but they were too far off to make out what was being said.

Jim whispered "We need to get closer and see what's under that tarp. Help me while I try to loosen this vent cover without making much noise."

Jim handed the machine gun to Mary and motioned to her to slide as far to her right as she possibly could. He turned his body in the small vent shaft until his feet were up against the vent cover. He gave one more look at Mary, who gave him the thumbs up sign that all was clear. He pushed against the vent cover with all his leg strength causing the vent cover to break loose and start to fall. Mary skillfully grabbed the cover before it fell to the floor. They were only four feet above the floor surface but if the cover had hit the floor it would have caused enough noise to alert, whoever was inside, to their presence.

Carefully Jim slid his feet out the open shaft and lowered them until they touched the floor. He stood up and took the vent cover from Mary's hands lowering it quietly to the floor. He retrieved the weapon from Mary and assisted her out onto her feet. Jim carefully slid the vent cover back into place then the two of them hurriedly crossed the short six foot distance from the vent to a small opening in the tarp that was covering the mysterious figure inside the hangar. Cautiously he opened the flap wide enough where he and Mary could step in carefully and closed the flap behind them. The light inside was dim but thanks to several small openings in the tarps slit the lighting was good enough to make out the object under it.

Jim was stunned. Mary noticed the drastic change in his demeanor and whispered to him "What is it?"

Chapter XIV

Conveniently disguised with desert camouflage, a private Leer jet gently floated down from the ever darkening evening sky. Stars were beginning to sparkle like glitter across the eastern horizon as the private passenger jet rolled to a stop. Sam Young looked out his jet window and read the words, welcome to Southeastern Arizona, Sierra Vista Army Air Terminal. The turbine engines were winding down to a stop when Tim Walker and Henry Steel approached the jet as the door hatch was being opened and the steps lowered.

Sam Young appeared in the small doorway and Tim Walker wondered how Sam's 6 foot, 1 inch, 230lb frame could exit the small plane doorway with such ease. Henry Steel leaned over a bit toward Tim and whispered "He's looking a lot older, is he feeling alright?"

Tim noticed the change also but tried to nullify Henry's comment by replying "You'd look old too if you had been in this business for nearly forty years.

Sam was in this business ten years before there even was a CIA."

When Sam approached the pair of agents he said in his deep baritone voice "Tim! Henry! It's good to see the both of you. Where do we stand in this Miller business?"

Tim spoke first "Well sir, our last signal we received from the tracking device, we hid on Mary's plane, indicated they had landed at a small airstrip in the Sonora Desert fifteen miles east of Puerto Penasco. Our Mexican friends tell us there is a small group of German people there. They tell us the Germans are holding about four or five Americans. The leader of the group is a female who, our informants, say answers to the name of Hilda."

Sam smiled with the satisfaction of knowing his explanation to his superiors of this whole situation was right. Now he had the enjoyment of introducing his idea of how they were going to end this threat.

Sam turned toward the plane and said "Gentleman, I want you to meet someone who will stop Hilda and her Nazi gang."

Suddenly a tall figure appeared in the jets doorway. Tim and Henry looked at each other with a puzzled look then looked over at Sam for an explanation.

"Gentlemen I want you to meet General Mueller, he was a World War II ex-Nazi general and commander of the Third German Panzer division. He also is a retired secret agent from MI-6 and father of Hilda Mueller."

Tim and Henry were dumbstruck. Neither one of them could say a word. Henry finally broke the stunned silence when he said "But Sir! I thought he was dead!"

Sam always enjoyed springing these surprises on his field agents. He felt it gave them an attitude adjustment and taught them a lesson about how young field agents should never underestimate the abilities of an older agent. Sam knew how they were starting to think of him as an old washed up agent and he hoped this surprise would change their way of thinking

General Mueller slowly descended the jets stairs to ground level. Tim couldn't help but notice the Generals six foot two inch height. He was standing up straight as a stiff military statue. Only decades of self-discipline could create such a distinct human being. Tim noticed the cane the general was holding in his right hand and how detailed its carved designs were. The general noticed Tim's interest in it and said "I stole it from the Eagles nest in Austria. Hitler had it specially made as a gift for Himmler's birthday way back in nineteen forty five. Unfortunately the war ended before his birthday and I figured neither one of them needed it anymore. So, when I received orders to meet the American Army in Salzburg and show them the way to Hitler's lair I did what they asked and reaped some of its rewards."

Tim also noticed the General was favoring his right leg, stirring his imagination to wonder if it was an old war injury and if it was, how did it happen? Tim looked into the Generals hard, cold, blue eyes and felt a chilling stare that penetrated deep into his soul where it struck a chord of fear. Tim wondered how many others had felt that same sense of fear. He also noticed the strong granite like cheek bones and his stern clean shaved chin. It did seem a little strange for the general to be wearing an old gray trench coat. What really puzzled Tim the most was that Swiss Alpine hat the general was wearing with a small feather in the left side of the hatband. Somehow that just didn't fit into the American southwest desert.

Tim's thoughts were interrupted by Henry when he heard him address Sam. "Sir we need to get over to the helipad. We have a Huey standing by waiting for your orders to proceed into Mexico. There's two more nearby filled with platoons of special ops troops who will follow us down and engage the enemy if it comes to that. Did we get permission from the Mexican government to enter?"

"Yes," Sam replied over the loud noise of the Huey cranking up its engine. "The Mexican government said they will be standing by if we need assistance. We'll be going in dark and flying low, no lights on the choppers. I don't want to be spotted before we get there. Once we get there Henry, I want you to take one platoon around to the north side of the runway. Tim! I need you to take another platoon around to the south end of the runway. I have Captain Conner taking a third platoon and landing about a half mile to the west of the hangar. The general and I will be taking a platoon in from the east. Be careful and don't shoot unless you are shot at. We have hostages down there and one of them is my God son."

The Hueys motor increased in speed lifting its heavy load off the pad. As it smoothly rose to its flight elevation the pilot gently pushed the stick slightly forward and the Huey headed south. The constant humming of the choppers engine was temporally interrupted by the pilot's voice crackling over the head set to the other pilots. "We're going to run with our lights on until we reach the Mexican border, then we will go dark and fly below the radar until we reach our destination."

The other pilots replied "Roger that Bill! It looks like we're in for a long night."

The sun had set and the blanket of stars, shining brightly above the choppers, gave each man on board a false sense of peace. The bright, half-moon was just beginning to peek above the eastern horizon, emitting light the chopper pilots needed to help guide them across the Sonora Desert to what could be, for some, their final destination. Sam, strapped to his seat, watched out the open hatch of the Huey as the moons light created long shadows of the three fingered saguaro cactus on the sandy desert floor. He prayed they would be able to get to their destination and complete the mission without any losses. He silently hoped they weren't already too late to rescue the hostages. Sam thought about Mary and Jim and knew if they could get free from their captives they would be trying to wreak havoc from the inside. Sam's real worry was for Annie, Cody, and JP. He wondered if they were still being held captive or had they been killed? Was Cody able to evade detection hiding in the plane Mary had landed and was he able to escape with JP and Annie? The worry weighed heavy on Sam's mind as the chopper flew south and disappeared into the darkness.

Chapter XV

I could see the stress and tired look on Annie's face as we rested near a group of Joshua trees. It has been nearly twenty four hours now since this whole disaster had started and Annie had been caring for JP the entire time. I knew she had to be on the edge of total exhaustion. JP was asleep in my arms while Annie lay curled up on the sandy desert floor resting her head on my lap. I estimated we had crossed, roughly, a mile or maybe two since leaving Jim and Mary back at the kidnapper's secret airstrip.

I gazed up at the stars in the clear night sky and noticed the half-moon had crossed over to the western half of the sky. I worried we might be caught out in the open when the sun came up. I knew if we were, our survival chances would be impeded. If the kidnappers caught us again I felt certain it would be a short capture, but for Annie' and JP, it would be torturous. I glanced at my watch. It had been twenty minutes since we first stopped to rest and my senses were telling me we needed to be up and moving as far away from that airport and as fast as we could go. If there were any pursuers on our trail it wouldn't take them long to catch up to us.

I gently put my hand on Annie's shoulder and said softly "Sweetheart, it's time for us to move out."

When I said "it's time to move out" a flashback, from my days in Vietnam, entered my memory. I could picture in my mind the six of us, Rick, Louis, CJ, Sam, Tom, and I, grabbing our gear and heading out on patrol. Seeing them in my memory brought back the heartache of having lost Louis and Rick to a nighttime attack, on the NCO club the same evening I was there proposing to Annie. I quickly shook off the painful memory; but the pain of loss will always be with me.

Annie started to rise up from her resting position but instantly froze in place with fear. I too, had heard the sound of a foot step nearby and quietly slipped out the 32 special I had tucked away under my belt and silently got it ready for action. The sound Annie and I had heard was familiar to the both of us. It was the same sound we had often heard on our gravel driveway back home in Colorado. The distinct, unmistakable crunch, a boot or a shoe, makes when walking on loose gravel.

Annie looked at me with a slight fear in her eyes. I put my finger up to my lips indicating to her not to speak. I gently handed JP over to her and started to ease my way up off the ground. I stood between her and the direction of the noise when a deep voice from the darkness said. "Herr Miller, if you don't want to see the fraulein die then don't move another centimeter! Now Herr Miller, very carefully set the pistol down and place your hands behind your head!"

I carefully laid the pistol down, but as I did, I said in a loud voice "Don't shoot! I'm laying the gun down."

When I did, I placed it directly in front of Annie who was still sitting down holding JP. Annie looked at me and without a word being said she knew what I was going to do and what she had to do.

I stood the rest of the way up raising my hands above my head so the kidnapper could see them clearly in the moonlight. The kidnapper stepped out from behind a large saguaro with his AK47 pointed directly at me.

Annie recognized him right away. It was Herman Kessler, Hilda's youngest son. She remembered him all too well. He had those evil eyes that gave her cold chills. She knew what he wanted and she knew he was going to kill Cody to get it.

I stepped to my left to block Herman's view of Annie and JP. When I did Annie reached out quickly and grabbed the pistol I had laid down in front of her and quickly pulled it back, hiding it under JP's cover.

JP who was cradled in her right arm started to wake up and cry, but Annie gently patted him and whispered "Shhh, it will be alright." Using the distraction of JP's cry gave Annie the time she needed to lift the pistol, still hidden under the baby's blanket, and point it at the approaching Herman without raising his suspicion.

Herman stepped forward, appearing out of the shadow of a saguaro. He kept a cautious watch on me and a nervous trigger finger on his AK-47 just daring me to make a wrong move. The tension in the air was heavy. I knew when Herman looked at the spot where I had laid the pistol down in front of Annie and not see it he probably would shoot me. What I was betting on, though was, due to the moons shadows crisscrossing our resting area he wouldn't be able to see it. I also understood that if Herman were to figure out who had it he would, without hesitation, kill all of us. I had an idea and knew what I needed to do. I moved, with my hands above my head, slowly and carefully, further away from Annie and JP while continuing a conversation with Herman. I knew that irritating Herman would distract him enough to possibly forget about the pistol.

I began by saying: "So! Hermee, what's it like having an insane mother who is wanted by nearly every country in the world?"

I smiled knowing Herman would get upset with

the way I degraded his mother. Right now I only hoped Herman wouldn't get too upset and pull the trigger. I understood enough about psychology that when you toy with a person's feelings there is a fine line that you need to walk. If you cross over it too far it could end instantly in disaster.

Herman stepped closer to our group. He felt his anger start to build toward the sarcastic way this disgusting American was treating his family. He wanted to pull the trigger and kill this arrogant American immediately but for right now, he would control his anger and make this ignorant American suffer.

Keeping his feelings under control, Herman replied, "How did you know who I vas? Dummkoph!"

"That was easy." I replied as I kept moving cautiously away from JP and Annie hoping to get Herman to continue facing me with his back toward Annie.

"I was on the train in Colorado, dressed up as a porter, asking everyone if they wanted a drink. You didn't notice me because you kept staring at my wife which, proves you have good taste, but, also proves your ignorance."

Herman's trigger finger started tapping the trigger of his AK-47as he said "Vas do you mean calling me ignorant?"

I realized he was now in the position I wanted him to be in. Herman had stepped between me and Annie with his backside facing Annie. I thought 'This guy's dumber then he looks or he thinks Annie's not a threat to him.'

I could see Annie as she slowly laid JP off to her right side onto the soft, warm, sand and raise the pistol in her left hand pointing it at the back of Herman's head.

"Well Hermiee, if you had any intelligence at all, you would have picked up the pistol I laid down on the sand but now it's too late. If I were you and I had a woman pointing a pistol at the back of my head I'd not move a finger, if you know what I mean."

Herman thought about it a second then heard a familiar click, from behind his head. It was a sound he had heard many times before when he and his family were out honing their shooting skills. Only this time the sound of a gun being cocked ready to fire came with a soft voice that sent sudden fear, with embarrassment, racing through his body. *He thought, 'How could I have been so stupid not to have remembered that gun?'*

Annie said in a soft voice, "Herr Herman, if you so much as move an eyelash you'll never blink again. If you want to see your mother once more then you had better do what I say. Put your rifle safety to the on position and carefully lower it to the ground. Don't even think for a second, that I can't use this pistol. The 55 grain, hollow point rounds, with its hair trigger, will blow your head clean off. Needless to say, it has been a very long day for me and I'm tired and nervous. Any sudden moves could cause my finger to twitch on this hair trigger creating, for you, an end to a very tragic life."

Herman didn't move as his mind raced at lighting speed with thoughts on how he could win this stand-off. He knew the moment he took his rifle off Cody it would be all over for him. He only had seconds to think about what he would do before Annie would shoot. Or would she? The man was at least five steps from him and the woman was within arms' length behind him. If he spun around fast enough he could knock the pistol out of her hand. Then kick her down with his foot while at the same time, spin back around, just in time to shoot the man who would, without a doubt, be coming at him.

Herman had a big ego that gave him a lot of self-confidence and a great feeling of calmness and self-control as he said to himself "NOW!"

Chapter XVI

Three hundred yards to the north, just beyond a tall cactus covered rise, three black helicopters, flying in whisper mode, landed with two dozen special ops troops recruited and trained by the CIA. Out of one, offloaded Sam Young, Tim Walker, Henry Steel, and ex-Nazi General, AKA, MI-6 spy Hrolf Muller. The chopper engines were quiet and the blades had stopped spinning as the sixteen men headed west across the desert towards the enemy airstrip a little more than a half mile away. Sam Young and special ops group leader Second Lieutenant Sam Coldwater, a recruit from OCS (officer candidate school) by Sam Young, had climbed to the top of a small rise. From there they looked west, through binoculars, at the few distant lights coming from the airstrip. Suddenly, from their left flank, they heard two shots ring out. Having served in Vietnam Lieutenant Coldwater was familiar with the sound of individual weapons. He determined the shots came from a 32 caliber pistol and an AK-47 at approximately 300 yards distance.

SEARCH FOR ANNIE

"Sir" Lieutenant Coldwater whispered to Sam Young "That was the sound of an AK-47 and a small caliber pistol. I recognize the sound of the AK from my days in Nam. You don't suppose those shots were made by enemy spotters sending a warning signal do you?"

Sam thought for a few moments and said "Lieutenant, take two men and check it out. We'll wait here fifteen minutes then move out toward the airstrip. We need to get their just before sunrise"

"Yes sir, I'll take Jefferies and Michaels with me."

Without saying another word Lieutenant Coldwater turned to his squad and pointed at Jefferies and Michaels, signaling to them by hand jester, to follow him. The three men moved out quietly, heading in the direction of the gunshots.

Lieutenant Sam Coldwater was a tall broad shouldered man in his early twenties with coal black hair and deep brown eyes. His mother and father, who owned a large cattle ranch in Oklahoma, were of American Indian heritage. Sam also had three other brothers who worked on the ranch helping their parents. One brother had a crippled leg he received when he was injured in a bull riding contest at a local rodeo event.

Sam Coldwater was a quiet no nonsense leader. After his tour in Nam was over he felt something was missing in his life and decided to reenlist for officers training. His disciplined attitude and high grades, in

OCS, caught the attention of agent Sam Young. Sam, who himself, attended that same school many years before admired Sam Coldwater's knowledge and understanding of guerilla warfare. He impressed the agency so much that they decided to offer him a position as an Ops officer in the CIA when he graduated. Now, four weeks after graduation young Second Lieutenant Coldwater was leading a life that filled the void he felt when he flew out of Vietnam for the last time.

The three men quietly approached the general area where they had estimated the gunshots had been fired. Lieutenant Coldwater raised his hand and motioned to his two men to halt. Kneeling in the desert sand he listened for any unusual sounds. At first he didn't hear anything except the early morning breeze creating a slight whisper as it flowed softly through the desert Joshua trees that were all around them. Then, faintly he heard what sounded like a baby crying. The Lieutenant looked over at Jefferies and Michaels. The look on their faces suggested they were in disbelief as much as he was. Sam waved the trio cautiously forward.

The closer they got to the crying sound of a baby the more cautious they became. Each of them wondered 'Was this a trap? Was this some elaborate hoax by the enemy to draw them into an ambush?' Despite all their natural instincts telling them not to go, they moved forward anyway. They knew when they took the oath to serve and protect the United States of America from all its enemies; it was their job to do just that.

Lieutenant Coldwater motioned for Michaels and Jefferies to stay put while he moved into a position where he could see into the clearing. Sam slowly crawled forward and peered around the base of a Joshua tree into the clearing where the baby was crying. He could see the baby lying in the sand near the base of a Joshua tree. Not too far away lay another body that looked as if it could be a man. Sam motioned to Jefferies and Michaels to move around to the west where, on his signal, they would rush into the clearing at the same time with the hope to surprise whoever was hiding there. Within a few minutes Michaels and Jefferies were in position. Lieutenant Coldwater gave his signal and the trio charged into the clearing. Finding no resistance Sam went over to the crying baby while Jefferies and Michaels checked out the man's body.

Michaels quickly checked the man for a pulse and said "He's still alive Lieutenant, it looks as if a bullet grazed his head, but he seems to be ok otherwise."

"Good, see if you can find any I.D. on him while I try to help the baby. Jefferies! Use the radio and contact Sam Young, tell him what we've found. Let him know our cover may have been blown and we'll catch up to him at the airstrip after we transport our two victims to the chopper."

RON MAHAFFEY

Lieutenant Coldwater noticed there were two other tracks in the sand. He determined by their number, size, and depth of the depressions, there were only two people who got away. One, according to its foot size, appears to be a female. Sam spotted the baby's bag and searched it for anything that would help the child. He found a half filled bottle and tested it to make sure it was safe to feed the baby. Michaels found the man's wallet and had turned to hand it to the Lieutenant when he watched him tip the baby bottle up and allowed a little of its content to drip into his mouth.

"Yuck! That's sick Lieutenant! For all you know that could be poisoned."

Sam could see the look on Michaels face and chuckled as he replied "Private, I was raised on a ranch in Oklahoma and my brothers and I ate and tasted a lot worse than this. What did you find?"

"I found his wallet sir."

Sam placed the bottle in the baby's mouth which the baby began to happily drain as fast as the nipple would allow. The baby quieted down to enjoy his meal as Sam turned to Michaels and said "What does his I.D. show?"

Michaels pulled out the victims I.D. and replied "Well sir, it says he is from Colorado and his name is Cody Miller."

Sam almost dropped the baby when he heard the

name. He hurriedly handed the baby over to Michaels and quickly knelt down beside Cody. Using the moonlight he looked closer at Cody's face and started to laugh.

"Well I'll be the son of a monkey's uncle; Private Michaels I want you to meet my old Vietnam platoon sergeant and good friend Cody Miller. I always wondered what happen to him after we were bombed and shelled while in that NCO club at Cu-Chi. He had just proposed to one of the base nurses. Annie was her first name. I don't remember her last but I'll bet this is their baby".

"Looks like we'll find out real soon Lieutenant, he's beginning to wake up."

I could feel my senses begin to return life to my injured and stunned body. I could hear talking and feel a terrific pain in my head as my mind began to function again. Then, in a speed of light, my memory of what had just happened to me exploded in my mind and I yelled "ANNIE!" as I tried to sit up. I felt someone's hand on my shoulder holding me down.

I started to fight when I tried to get up but heard a deep familiar voice say "Easy Sergeant Miller, you've been wounded again but you'll be alright in a few minutes. So take it easy for a few moments."

I began to recognize a voice from my past but, what

was confusing me, is how did I end up back in Vietnam again or had I ever left? Could I be dreaming all this? The pain I felt in my head was real. I slowly opened my eyes but my vision was still blurry. I could see three dark figures against the background of a moonlit sky but the details were still a little fuzzy. I looked around and could see the Joshua trees and smell the warm sandy desert floor. Reality was back and my memory of everything that had taken place over the last couple of days returned. Who was behind that voice that seemed so familiar?

I began to sit up when the familiar voice once again said "Sarge take it easy in getting up. You probably have a mild concussion from the bullet that grazed your head."

My foggy memory was beginning to clear when I asked in a questionable tone "Sam, is that you?"

"It sure is Sarge. It's been awhile my friend." Sam replied with a big grin on his face.

Jefferies began to wrap Cody's head wound as Cody asked "What on God's green earth are you doing down here in this Mexican desert?"

"Never mind that now." replied Sam "what we need to find out from you is, do they know we are here?"

I was still feeling a bit dazed as I said "They have Annie and my son, we need to go after them before they get away!"

"Calm down Cody, private Michaels is holding

your son. He seems to be alright and I've spotted tracks heading in the direction of the airstrip, but what we need to know is do they know we are here?"

"No, not yet, but we need to get to the airstrip in a hurry."

Sam turned to Jefferies and said "Private, I need you to take the baby back to the chopper. When you get there, stay with him until we return. Take the baby's bag with you and see if you can find something to feed him. Tell the chopper pilot to stand by and when the time is right we'll meet up with him at the airstrip. Got that?"

"Yes sir!" Jefferies answered as he took the baby from Michael's arms, slung the baby's bag over his shoulder and headed back to the chopper. Jefferies was a natural when it came to caring for children. He was the oldest of eight children, five brothers and three sisters. He helped his mother raise his brothers and sisters after his father died when his single engine plane crashed. It happened in a corn field outside of Omaha, Nebraska, while he was dusting crops. Jefferies was twelve at the time and went to work for a local farmer plowing his fields and caring for the animals. He stood six foot tall and was a good looking boy with blond hair, green eyes with an average build. Jefferies common sense and total understanding of his responsibilities gave Lieutenant Coldwater a clear understanding of why he could trust Jefferies to follow his orders to the letter.

I watched Jefferies disappear into the desert carrying my son. I felt my heart ache with loss but I knew JP would be safe now and I could concentrate on getting Annie back.

I then looked over at Sam with a puzzled look and said "Sir?"

Sam smiled and replied "It's a long story I'll tell you later. Right now we need to get to that airstrip. Michaels! Grab the radio and let's move out. Notify our leader that we have rescued two hostages and are heading to the airstrip."

I was anxious to try and catch up to Annie so I quickly picked up the 32 off the desert sand. I brushed the sand off of it and tucked it behind my belt. The 32 had fallen when Herman performed a surprise karate move by instantly spinning and kicking the pistol out of Annie's hand causing the gun to fire. Almost at the same time, Herman fired his rifle at me before I could even take a step. Lucky for me the shot was off just enough to only graze my head.

I said "Let's move out, I'll take the lead."

Sam smiled as he moved up beside me and whispered "Don't worry Sarge, we'll get her back."

The three of us headed west back across the desert, toward the airstrip. The eastern horizon was beginning to show a thin line of daylight. That little voice in my head kept telling me to hurry, time was running out.

Chapter XVII

Mary and Jim stood quietly under the tarp that covered the missile, watching the light glare coming from the four inch gap between the floor and the bottom edge of the tarp. Their eyes were fixed on the shadow created by one of the security guards as he slowly walked by them oblivious to Jim and Mary's presence just inches away. When the shadow disappeared Mary breathed a quiet sigh of relief and whispered "What is this thing?"

Jim whispered back, "A Russian made ballistic missile or as the military calls it, an ICBM. It's capable of wiping out an entire U.S. city within a 5500 mile radius. From here they could attack any city from LA to San Diego to Austin, Texas. Back in sixty three the Russians had several of these things parked in Cuba just ninety miles south of Key West. You remember how that turned out."

"Yes" Mary softly replied "It nearly started World War III. How did these Nazis get one and what's it doing here?"

Jim whispered close to Mary's ear. "My suspicion is the Nazis made a deal with a Russian black market arms dealer to sell them the Inner-Continental Ballistic Missile. He probably agreed only with the stipulation that they target a U.S. city. The Russians are in need of a lot of cash to start drilling for oil in Siberia. The oil will eventually bring them trillions of dollars in revenue. At the same time the Nazi attack would pay back the U.S. for embarrassing Russia in front of the whole world, when we forced them to back down in the Cuban crisis. Plus, if one of their missiles incinerates one of our cities the Russians can blame the whole incident on the Nazis. The Russians will then claim their innocence, thereby increasing their influence over the European countries by showing them our weakened economy and lack of security."

Mary and Jim stood quietly under the missile tarp and listened to the various noises and chatter going on around them. They knew that one tiny noise from their location would bring death for the both of them. As they stood there hundreds of thoughts raced through their minds. Did Annie, Cody, and JP escape? Had Sam been notified and was he now on his way to rescue them? Where was Hilda and how do we destroy this missile before they launch it?

Jim whispered to Mary "Wait here."

SEARCH FOR ANNIE

She watched him as he moved ever so slowly to the overlapping seam in the tarp. Gently, using one finger, he slipped the one edge of the tarp slightly open, just far enough to see towards the end of the missile. He could see two or three men wearing white lab coats. One of them was walking around looking at the instrument panel on the missile. Another was writing something down on a clipboard and returning to some location on the other side of the missile. He slowly closed the tarp edge to its original position and quietly returned to Mary's location.

Jim softly said "I've got to see what's on the other side of this missile."

He gently slipped by Mary and passed under the missile warhead to the other side. He started, cautiously, to open the tarp when he heard a door fling open, with a loud bang followed by an equally booming noise as it slammed shut. Immediately following was an earsplitting female voice saying "Where the hell is my son Herman and why hasn't any of my security people found the escapee's yet? If these prisoners have gotten away someone is going to pay dearly for it!"

Just at that moment the door to the missile hangar flew open again and in walked Herman.

Hilda seeing him instantly screamed "WHERE HAVE YOU BEEN?"

Herman smiled as he reached outside the door,

grabbing Annie's wrist and jerking her inside and flinging her to the floor. Annie could feel the stress of the day and the wear on her aching body as she slowly got up off the floor and stood up.

She instantly turned to Herman and angrily slapped him just as hard as she could. Herman was caught by surprise at her bold move as he staggered backward.

Annie glared with hatred at him and said "If I find my baby and husband dead I will personally see that you suffer a slow agonizing death!"

Herman, still feeling the sharp sting of the slap said "Here mother, I have brought you an early Christmas gift."

Hilda laughed when she saw the slap and said "How ironic this is. It was thirty years ago in another hangar in another part of the world that I slapped your mother in the very same way."

Hilda's eyes narrowed like a venomous cobra as she slithered across the floor of the hangar toward Annie. Watching her slowly approach, Annie began to feel the fear she had felt only once before. It was that night nearly three years ago when she and Cody were in the NCO club on their base in Vietnam with bombs dropping all around them. The fear flashed pictures of Cody's last desperate measure as he leaped across the table pushing her to the floor just as the bomb exploded inside the club and everything went black. This time she took the fear she was feeling and gradually turned it into hate, as Hilda neared. Annie thought about her son, who was left out in the desert, vulnerable for any wild animal to freely consume. She remembered seeing Cody lying there in the desert sand with blood running down his face. While Herman, with a tight viselike grip around her wrist, drug her away. She wondered if the bullet fired from Herman's rifle killed the man she so desperately loved. The closer Hilda got to her the more the fear turned to anger, then to hatred.

When Hilda got to Annie she expected to see fear but was surprised to see hatred in her eyes. It pleased her to know she had hurt Maria's daughter.

Hilda hissed "We've got them now! Wait till they hear we have their daughter. They will come begging me to kill them and let her go, but, I'll kill them all. Good job son! What happen to the others?"

When Mary heard Hilda's remark the hair on the back of her neck stood up. She could feel her blood starting to boil. She looked over at Jim and whispered "I'm going out there. They have Annie, I can't let them hurt my little girl."

Jim put his hand on Mary's shoulder and motioned to her with his other hand to calm down. He whispered to her "Give me just a few more minutes I have a plan that may get us all out of here safely."

Herman's pride in what he had done for his mother

boosted his ego to the point of adding exaggeration to his story. He told his mother what happened to the rest of Annie's family. He smiled and explained to Hilda with pride. "I killed her husband and left the child out in the desert to be eaten by the coyotes."

Hilda grabbed Herman and gave him a hug and said "I'm proud of you son. The Furor will be happy with the way you've turned out."

Just at that moment the door to the hangar came open. In walked Hilda's husband Adolf and her older son Martin who was helping his elderly grandfather, ex-Major Kessler.

Hilda immediately announced "Look what our son Herman has brought to his mother for a Christmas gift." Then with a sinister glare she added "What have you three brought for me?"

Adolf and Martin were silent with embarrassment but old man Kessler was not teetered by Hilda's attitude. He said "Get off your high horse Hilda and tell me what time this missile is set to go off?"

Hilda refrained from further exploitation of her personal grudge against the Wilsons and said "Major, according to our spies in Washington, the President's plane is to land at San Clemente, California, at 9AM. Thirty minutes later we are to fire our missile at his residence. As long as this Russian made piece of junk does what we paid for and strikes close to the target we should have a kill. The Third Reich will be feared by the world again and our Furor will have his revenge and we will have earned the worlds respect."

Standing there with Herman tightly grasping her wrist, Annie knew she had to do something to stop this madwoman from destroying the world. She glanced around the hangar and quickly estimated it to be the size of a football field with a 40 foot ceiling. She noticed a catwalk about the twenty foot level that ran around the entire inside of the hangar. She spotted a seam in the center of the ceiling that ran the entire length of the hangar. She also noticed what appeared to her, to be a huge hydraulic piston at each corner and two more that were centered on each side of the building.

She remembered seeing a smaller version of a hydraulic piston used to lift the load bucket up on their ranch tractor back home in Colorado. The thought of home made her heart sink as she wondered if she, Cody, and JP would ever see it again.

She remembered seeing her home blown away and burning when her kidnappers drove by on their way out of the valley to escape capture. All the thoughts and pictures in her mind, of the day's events, came to a crashing halt. She spotted a rifle, unattended, leaning by itself up against a large wooden crate only fifteen feet away. She was familiar with its caliber and how to use it because Cody had bought one at a gun show they attended last spring in Denver. He had made a special point to train her on how to use it safely. Annie was devising a plan in her head about how she was going to get that rifle and what she would do next. Suddenly, from under the edge of the tarp she spotted the movement of someone's shoe. It was barely visible and probably wouldn't have been noticed if she hadn't been looking right at that spot when it moved. She casually looked away for a moment just in case someone nearby was watching her. She hoped there wasn't a change in her facial expressions that anyone noticed.

Looking around at the group near her no one else seemed to have noticed. Everyone else was listening to the madwomen explain their next move. She glanced back toward the shoe and it was gone, but so was the rifle. A calm demeanor came over her as she felt the shoe could only have belonged to one person, her father. She knew something was about to happen and felt comfort in knowing that her mother and father were close by.

Chapter XVIII

Lieutenant Coldwater and I arrived at the agreed upon position located three hundred yards east of the hangar. The sun wasn't up yet but the gray morning light was getting brighter. We spotted Agent Young, lying, belly down in the sand, behind a large saguaro cactus looking through a pair of binoculars toward the hangar. We stayed low as we crept up beside him.

Lieutenant Coldwater said "Sir, we were able to rescue two of the captives. One was a baby who I sent back to the helo with Private Jefferies and the other is here with me. I want you to meet my old platoon sergeant Cody…"

Before Lieutenant Coldwater could finish his sentence Agent Sam turned and said "It's good to see you again Cody, how's that head wound?"

Lieutenant Coldwater was flabbergasted. "Well I'll be an old mule skinner! You two know each other?"

I smiled and said "Yes we do, Agent Sam here was at my wedding. He helped Annie track me down last year when I was determined to leave, this so called, civilization behind and live out the rest of my life as a mountain man."

I could tell that left the Lieutenant with more questions to ask but I looked at him and said "Later my friend, both of us have a lot to talk about."

I turned to Sam Young and described everything that had happened in the last twenty four hours. I told him of the ten to fifteen heavily armed troops in and around the hangar. I told him that I believe Mary and Jim were trying to get inside the hangar and I hadn't heard anything that would indicate otherwise. I don't believe they have been caught yet. I also told him Annie had been captured and the leader of the group was called Hilda. I was relaying all of my information to Sam when I noticed an elderly gentleman lying on the desert sand nearby listening closely to my every word.

I stopped talking and asked "Who's that?"

Sam Young smiled and said "Cody I want you to meet ex-Nazi General Hrolf Mueller, AKA, Agent C.J. Tuttle from the British Intelligent agency called, MI-6. He is Hilda's father."

I went numb, I didn't know whether to shake the man's hand or shoot him.

Agent Tuttle could see the look in Cody's eyes when Agent Sam told Cody who he was. He understood the confusion that was going on in Cody's mind. He began by saying in his strong British accent "I'm deeply sorry Ole man, for all the trouble my daughter has given you and your family. MI-6 and I have been chasing her for years. This is the first time we have come this close to catching her. Now with your help, we will give it our all to get your family out alive."

Cody's feelings were confused but he realized Annie and family came first. He cautiously shook Tuttle's hand and said "Let's finish it today."

Sam Young was back lying on the top edge of the sand dune. He was watching the hangar through his binoculars. Slowly he lowered them and slipped down below the top edge out of sight from the hangar. He turned his head toward Cody and said "This is what we have planned right now. Agent Tuttle has agreed to go in first, alone. We figure it will throw all of them for a loop and confuse their plans for a few moments while we move in. Our people are in position to take out the outside security guards when we give them the word. I'm not sure what they have inside the hangar but Agent Tuttle is wearing a listening devise. We'll know everything that goes on in there and judge from what we hear, when it would be good to go in."

Cody directed a question toward agent Tuttle "What will you tell them when they ask how you got here?"

Tuttle replied "Hilda is a smart women, she will

have figured it out the minute she sees me, that I didn't come alone."

Tuttle looked around and added "The sky is getting lighter, we need to move now."

Tuttle looked at Agent Young and said "Sam, it's time. Tell your point men to take out their targets."

Cody listened intently for any sound of gunfire but only heard the whisper of the wind blowing through the Joshua trees. Five minutes went by in silence, and then Cody heard the familiar crackling of static come over Lieutenant Coldwater's radio. A voice came over it whispering. "Three targets down, clear to advance."

I looked over toward agent Tuttle but the agent was already on the move toward the hangar. He had removed his trench coat and was wearing a Nazi Generals uniform. Agent Young notified all companies to move up within a hundred yards of the hangar and dig in. Cody knew he had to move immediately if he was going to save Annie. The suns tip was just peeking above the desert floor lighting up the east side of the hangar. I spotted what appeared to be an air vent into the hangar.

I started heading for it but was suddenly stopped by Lieutenant Coldwater who said "I'm going with you."

Then Sam Young stopped me and said "You two are going to need these." He handed me and Lieutenant Coldwater two, fully loaded, M-16's.

SEARCH FOR ANNIE

I said to my friend "You don't need to come on this patrol Lieutenant. This could be the one we don't come back from.

Lieutenant Sam said in a low voice "You're not leaving me behind Sarge; you need me for back up."

Ducking behind sand dunes and dodging between Joshua trees and saguaros Sam and I raced the last hundred yards, of the open airstrip, to the hangar's east side. Sam, who is an excellent tracker, noticed other footprints around the four foot by four foot air vent we were about to enter.

"Sarge, two other tracks are here and they look recent. Their foot print size indicates one could possibly be a female and the other is a male."

We entered the dark hole of the air vent and crept along its, approximate fifteen foot length and four foot diameter opening. We came to a wire screen blocking our exit into the hangar. We noticed the scrape marks around the inside edges of the metal frame where the screens braces were fastened. It indicated to us that someone had been through here earlier. I had a good idea who it might have been. We listened to the noise and voices coming from inside the hangar but couldn't make out what was being said. The distance from our vent to where the people in the hangar were, created a muffled echo we couldn't understand.

Sam carefully looked through the slim opening of

the vent slats. He tried to see around the inside of the hangar, as much as he possibly could, but his limited view lacked a lot of information we had hoped for.

He whispered to me "Can't see much of anything! There's a stack of large metal drums on our left, blocking my view. I do see a large object with a tarp over it. It's roughly ten feet straight ahead."

The lieutenant quietly pushed the vent cover out and gingerly set it on the ground. Our exit from the vent was protected by the stack of fifty gallon drums on our left. We quickly looked around and saw the canvas that was draped over an object thirty feet long and fifteen feet high.

Lieutenant Coldwater tapped me on my shoulder and whispered "Lets duck under the tarp and see what these Nazis are hiding."

I whispered back "Not yet, hold on just a few more minutes."

The fifty gallon drums, we were hiding behind, were stacked two high with just enough space between them for me to peek through. I looked toward the other end of the hangar and could see a group of people appearing to be having a heated debate. I estimated there was an open space about ten feet wide between us and the canvas cover. Just at that moment, the hangar door opened and in walked C.J. Tuttle or better known as General Muller, Hilda's father. With everyone's eyes focused on the General I quietly whispered to Sam "Now is the time, let's duck under the tarp." We sprinted the ten feet to the canvas and ducked between two overlapping flaps and stepped under its cover, lowering the flaps behind us. When we stood up we came face to face with the barrel of an AK-47.

"Cody!" Mary said in a surprised whisper "What are you doing here?"

Both of us breathed a sigh of relief as I whispered "They have Annie and I'm going to get her back."

With a worried look on her face Mary said "Where is JP?"

I whispered "I left him with a medic, who took him to the rescue chopper. The chopper is almost two clicks east of here. The General just came through the door as we ducked under this tarp."

Mary and Jim looked puzzled when Mary whispered "General who?"

I replied "Sam Young said his name is Mueller and he is Hilda's father. You know him?"

Jim and Mary whispered at the same time "We thought he was dead."

Lieutenant Coldwater interrupted "There seems to be a lot of silence right now." What is this thing we're standing under anyway?"

Jim was holding the rifle and trying to remember where he had seen the lieutenant before. When it dawned on him, he had seen the lieutenant when he and Sam Young were visiting the CIA training facility at Quantico, Virginia last spring. Jim remembered him because he was one of Sam Young's most promising students.

"Good to see you again Lieutenant. Jim whispered

I looked with surprise at Sam and whispered to him "When this is over you and I have to talk!"

Sam smiled and nodded his head in agreement.

Jim continued "I take it since you are here Lieutenant, that we have help here also?"

"Yes sir" Lieutenant Sam whispered "The place is surrounded."

Chapter XIX

General Muller knew the minute he stepped inside the hangar anything could happen. He was hoping his appearance would throw everyone inside into a stupefied shock. It should give him enough time to see how the situation was set up so when the shooting started he might have a chance to survive. He put his hand into his left coat pocket of his newly pressed Nazi General's uniform and grasped the 9mm Luger. Feeling it gave him a little comfort to know that if things didn't go well he could at least have the opportunity to go out fighting. Just before he turned the doorknob to go in he paused for a moment and took one last look around. The sun was almost above the eastern horizon chasing away the last of the night darkness. It painted a beautiful panoramic sunrise by turning the small puffy white clouds into gold and turning the numerous tall saguaros into black, three fingered silhouettes against its bright, light blue sky.

He took a deep breath of the cool morning air then

just before he turned the doorknob he whispered to himself "God Bless Queen and Country."

He pushed the door open and stepped inside. His eyes adjusted to the dimmer light quickly and he gazed around at the surprised look of shock and disbelief on Major Kessler's face and the pale, dumbfounded, look of disbelief on Hilda's. The reaction he was getting is what he had hoped for as he walked passed everyone and came face to face with Hilda. Hilda's eyes were as big as silver dollars and her mouth had dropped open in utter surprise. He looked over at Major Kessler, who he believed, was about to have a cardiac moment. He glanced around the hangar and spotted the tarp covering the missile and caught sight of Cody and Sam as they darted under it. He quickly counted five armed men not counting Hilda, her husband Adolf, Major Kessler and the two young men he assumed were his grandsons. He noticed Annie standing beside the youngest of his grandsons who had a tight grasp of her arm.

He looked back at Hilda and said with a German accent "Well my dear, no hug for der vater?"

Hilda stuttered as she tried to speak. She could feel her mouth move but couldn't seem to form the words she was thinking, into a sentence. Then as her mind began to come back from its shock she said. "How? Where did you? Am I seeing a ghost? I thought you were dead!"

SEARCH FOR ANNIE

General Mueller replied "Not hardly, it will take a lot more than a war to kill me."

Hilda stretched her arm out and touched him with her shaking finger. He was human alright, but as her senses started to return many questions were beginning to fly through her brain. Slowly, anger began to control her attitude as she raised her fist to strike him.

The general grabbed her arm before she could strike and said "Now Hilda darling don't you remember what I taught you about striking out in anger?"

Annie was watching quietly as this whole scenario went down. She remembered the story her mother and father had told her, several months back, about General Muller and how no one knew that he was a British spy for MI-6 during World War II. She also knew that no one in the hangar knew his background like she did. When the general glanced over at her she knew from the look in his eyes that help was not far behind. Seeing the general and remembering the feet she had seen, under the missile tarp earlier, gave her hope that this nightmare would soon end.

Hilda screamed "Guards! KILL HIM!"

Old Major Kessler, having come out of his shock of surprise hollered "HALT! No one move yet, not until we get some answers from the General."

Kessler, with the help of his cane, hobbled over to General Muller and moved his face two inches from the Generals, and asked "How did you get here and how did you find us?"

The General smiled as he said "You know something Franz? I never did like you. There was a time I could have killed you. It disturbs me I didn't!"

Kessler's rage grew as he angrily said "General I believe I will kill you myself but first I want to know how you knew we were here and how did you get here?"

The General knew there wasn't any need to delay this show down. He looked around at the five heavily armed soldiers in the room then turned to Hilda and said "Sweetheart, you are my daughter and I know you'll find this hard to believe. But I don't want to see you killed. Right now there are sixty five heavily armed commandos outside waiting on you and your comrades. I need you to throw your weapons down and all of you go out with your hands on your heads to surrender."

Hilda looked over at her husband Adolf and sharply nodded her head toward the hangar door indicating for him to go look outside. Adolf carefully opened the door and looked quickly around the outside. The first thing he noticed was the missing security guards, he had left posted, were missing. Adolf was feeling nervous as he scanned several yards out and spotted a few heads sticking up above the sand dunes all around the outside of the hangar. He noticed the sun was above the eastern

SEARCH FOR ANNIE

horizon. He glanced toward the south where the airplane that Maria had landed in earlier was still parked. He secretly wished he could get on it and leave all this behind. He knew he couldn't and slowly stepped back inside the hangar and shut the door. He looked over at Hilda and said "Darling, the outside guards are missing and I spotted several heads sticking up above the sand dunes. I believe he's telling the truth."

Hilda looked at her father with deep hatred for him spewing out of her eyes. "You cowardly traitor! If you think for a minute that your men will stop us from our goal you are sadly mistaken. We have been planning this for years. Now that we are only a few minutes from completing our assigned mission I can guarantee you that we will all die before we let you stop us from achieving our goal. Why couldn't you have died on the Russian front like all the other honorable Nazis? You bring dishonor and shame to me and your grandsons. Now I, Hilda Adolf Kessler, will show you, you miserable coward, what it takes to be a hero to the Third Reich. TAKE THE TARP OFF OUR WEAPON!" She yelled. "AND OPEN THE MISSILE DOORS!"

The four hydraulic pump motors kicked on and the pistons began driving the hangar roof open exposing everyone to a clear blue sky. Two men stepped over to the tarp and started to remove it. Suddenly, out from underneath it, came Mary with the sub-machine gun and Jim carrying an AK-47. The one Annie had spotted earlier leaning up against the missile tarp. They stood there for a few moments enjoying the look of shock and surprise on everyone's face. A deathly silence overcame the noise of bullets being chambered, trigger hammers being cocked, and weapons being lifted and aimed for killing. Hilda was dumbstruck when she saw Maria.

Hilda's look of surprise didn't last long as it slowly turned into a terrible smug grin of revenge. "Now my lifelong quest will be fulfilled." She said with a tone of ugly satisfaction.

Annie jerked her arm out of Herman's tight grasp and ran over to her mother. Mary and Jim, with their guns aimed at Hilda, casually approached General Mueller's position.

"MOM, DAD," Annie said as she carefully stayed out of the line of their fire and stepped behind them.

Mary asked, "Are you alright Sweetheart?" Annie replied with a notable irritation in her voice and a mean glare at Herman. "Yes mom, but I was forced to leave JP and Cody out in the desert and Cody was shot." She struggled to hold back her tears as she said "He may be dead."

Jim interjected "Don't worry about them Anne, both of them are doing fine and in a minute we'll have you out of here joining them."

"Well, what do you know." Hilda snarled as she glared with ugly hatred at Maria. "All these years I have been dreaming of this moment and now here it is. My quest for revenge will finally come true when I force you to watch the killing of your entire family."

Mary smiled as she said. "Unless you have become a complete idiot, you must have noticed Hilda dear, that we are also holding weapons. I believe there is only one person who will walk out of here alive today and I guarantee it isn't going to be you."

Every ones attention was focusing on the activity behind the missile. I whispered to Lieutenant Coldwater "Lets slip out from under the tarp on the other side of the missile. It has plenty of cover and we'll be able to cover my family from a better position. We can quickly crawl behind several of those large square wooden crates lined up along the west side of the hangar wall."

I led the way, staying close to the ground and crawling from one piece of cover to the next. Several minutes later we found ourselves in a good location on the west side of the hangar hiding behind a couple wooden crates. I found two crates that were separated far enough apart for us to view the group of people that were gathered around the rear of the rocket. I felt a bit of relief when I spotted Annie standing next to her mother about seventeen yards away.

Lieutenant Coldwater whispered "I sure hope your father-in-law's plan works. One small mistake and we all could die."

I whispered back "He's been in this business longer then you and I have been alive. I have every bit of confidence in him. Once I have Annie back let the chips fall where they may, I just want Annie alive and out of here."

Hilda saw the machine gun Maria was holding but that didn't stop her from walking closer to Maria. She stood there for a few moments looking Maria up one side and down the other before Mary said "Hilda, the years have not been good to you. You have really aged a lot."

Hilda chuckled and replied "Don't worry about me looking old I'm going to personally see to it that you won't get any older."

Out of nowhere Hilda brings up a semi-automatic 9mm pistol and points it at Mary's head.

Jim yelled with the sound of panic in his voice "WAIT! Don't shoot or we'll all die."

Hilda snarled back "Give me one good reason why I shouldn't pull the trigger?"

General Mueller stepped up and got between Maria and Hilda. Hilda looked her father in the eyes with blood killing anger "Get out of my way traitor or I'll shoot you first."

SEARCH FOR ANNIE

General Mueller pulled his Lugar out of his pocket and pointed it at Hilda's heart. "If there has to be any killing then let it stay in the family. We will die together."

Sam Young was listening to the conversation going on inside the hangar through a receiver in his ear with its signal coming from the transmitter bug he planted on General Mueller's uniform. Sam Young leaned over to his lead officer and said "This is going to happen quickly when it starts. If you hear a shot from inside the hangar, tell your men to move in quickly."

The commander nodded his head agreeing.

To everyone's relief Hilda lowered her pistol. The tension in the hangar eased a bit.

Hilda, staring straight into Jim Wilson's eyes said "This can wait a few more minutes. Besides, I want all of you to watch my weapon go off."

Hilda shouted. "Remove the rest of the tarp and raise the missile to firing position!"

While the technicians readied the missile for firing Mary, with her weapon pointing at Hilda, whispered to Annie "When the shooting starts you hit the ground and crawl to the nearest cover. Cody is over by the wooden crates with backup. They will be taking out the goons and your father and I will take out the Kesslers."

The three hundred foot long and approximately two hundred foot wide hangar started humming with activity. When the roof of the hangar was at its maximum open position Hilda ordered the missile to be raised to its vertical firing position. When the nose cone of the missile reached its erect launch position the nose could barely be seen at the top of the opened roof edges. Daylight started streaming in giving most of the people inside the hangar a feeling of a fresh new day. All except one.

Hilda shouted to her missile technicians "Start the twenty minute count down and verify the missiles co-ordinance!"

Jim couldn't wait any longer. Time was running out. He looked over at General Mueller who indicated he was ready. Glancing at Annie, who was standing next to her mother, and using his eyes he indicated to her to get ready to hit the floor. She immediately understood what he was trying to tell her.

Annie squeezed her mother's hand letting her know she understood. A lump began to grow in her throat as she realized this could be the last time she might ever see her parents alive.

Chapter XX

Outside the hangar Sam Young watched as the hangar roof opened and the missiles nose cone appeared. He had been listening to everything going on inside the hangar thanks to the small electronic bug he had placed on General Mueller's coat collar. He knew time was up. He couldn't wait any longer.

He pressed the key on his radio and said "Everyone close in! Remember, we have hostages inside. Act accordingly and good luck."

Sam Young pulled his forty five semi auto out of his shoulder holster and headed, with his squad, towards the hangar door.

Inside the hangar one of Hilda's watchdogs shouted "They are coming ma'am!"

Hilda shouted to her rocket techs "Put the missile on automatic and grab your weapons."

Hilda swung her pistol up and fired, point-blank

into her father's chest. General Mueller felt the blast from Hilda's pistol with the sudden shock and pain of the bullets penetration. He desperately tried to pull the trigger on his 9mm but his hand seemed to have gone cold and numb. He started to speak but couldn't form any words, his vision started to go dark as he felt himself fall to the floor as darkness closed in around him, then nothing

Hilda quickly turned her gun toward Maria and started to squeeze off a second shot but it was too late, Maria fired first hitting Hilda with two quick shots. Hilda felt the hard punch of the bullets hit her chest followed by instant weakness that numbed the muscles of her body as if she had been hit by a bolt of lightning. Hilda, with her gun pointing at Maria, tried to pull the trigger. The numbness she felt racing through her body was killing her nerve circuits causing confusion to her mind and weakness to her muscles. She noticed the light starting to dim and wondered why. She felt her legs buckle and her head hit the floor. Her last thought was 'why me?' then everything faded to black.

When I saw Hilda kill her father, Lieutenant Coldwater and I opened up with our M-16's from behind the wooden crates. We instantly opened fire on the five security guards first as they were diving for

SEARCH FOR ANNIE

cover. We nailed two of them right off the bat; they fell to the floor like rag dolls. Another one started to race out the hangar door but was shot dead by the commandos on the outside. Sam and I turned our firepower on the other two who had reached cover and started shooting back at us. I watched both of them go down as their bullets flew all around us creating a loud snapping sound as they passed through the thin corrugated sheet metal wall behind us. I saw Jim instantly open up firing as fast as his automatic would allow him. He was able to shoot Adolf on the first shot before he and Mary hit the floor. Annie hit the floor the second Hilda shot her father and belly crawled under the halftrack that held the missile. Major Kessler pulled out a hand grenade and had started to pull the pin out but a stray bullet cut through his hand and he dropped it. When the grenade hit the floor the pin popped the rest of the way out. Major Kessler tried to run but lost his balance when he tripped over Adolf's dead body. Mary and Jim saw the pin pop out of the grenade, when it hit the floor, and knew they only had seven seconds to get as far away as they could before it exploded. They almost made it to Annie's hiding place under the missile halftrack when the explosion happened.

Jim felt a hot burn enter his back and felt his legs buckle as he fell to the floor and everything went dark. I saw Mary grab her leg and fall. The hangar door had swung open just as the grenade, which was near the door, exploded. Sam Young had just stepped through that door when the blast happened. He took most of the blast which saved several of the commandos following close behind him. The entire fight lasted two minutes then silence fell over the hangar and the gun smoke started to clear. Lieutenant Sam and I rose up slowly from behind our cover and carefully moved over to the bodies lying all around the hangar. I spotted Annie trying to bandage up her mother's leg and saw her father lying motionless on the floor nearby. The Lieutenant took charge of the commandos coming into the hangar and shouted for the radio man to call in the medivacs

I rushed over to Annie to see if she was alright and if I could help her. She was trying desperately to stop the bleeding coming from her mother's leg and stabilize her condition so the medics could quickly evacuate her and her father to the nearest medical facility.

I asked "Is there anything I can do to help you?"

She was calm and professional, thanks no doubt to her military training and the experience she received during her service in a Vietnam M.A.S.H. unit.

She quickly replied "Get a stretcher for my mother then get her out of here. I'm going to check my father."

I got two medics, with a stretcher, to carry Mary out and then I turned back toward Annie as she worked skillfully over her father whose wounds seemed to be more serious.

I said, "I was watching you, when the shooting started, crawl under the halftrack for cover. That was the best place you could have gone. I knew you had a good chance of survival there. How's your father?"

"He's still breathing, his pulse is weak and he's losing blood. We need to get him to a hospital quickly."

I yelled over to Sam "Sam! We need a medic and stretcher over here ASAP!"

Sam responded immediately to my request. The medics showed up and assisted Annie in stabilizing Jim. Then they loaded him and Mary onto a medivac chopper. I could see the worry and concern on Annie's face.

I put my arms around her and said "These men are well trained. Like you, they perform their jobs fast and efficiently without hesitation, because they know that to delay could cost a life."

Annie and I watched as the chopper carrying her parents disappeared to the north.

I said "The chopper pilot told me they were flying the dead and wounded to a hospital in Tucson. We'll meet with your parents there."

I held Annie tightly in my arms and whispered in her ear "I love you."

I could feel her tension relax as she whispered to me "Please tell me this is finally over."

Annie and I turned to head back to the hangar when Lieutenant Sam Coldwater walked up to us.

"Hello Miss Anne, it has been a longtime since the last time we met."

Annie looked at me with a questionable look. I grinned and said "This is Sam Coldwater from Oklahoma. He was in my squad back in Nam."

Annie's memory returned as she said "Of course I remember. You were in the NCO club the night it was bombed. It's good to see you again Sam, I'm glad you made it home alive. It looks like you have done well with your life."

"Yes Ma'am it's good to see you again. Unfortunately I have to tell you that one of our casualties was Sam Young."

Annie and I felt as if a part of our family had died. We had made him JP's Godfather. He had a big hand in helping Annie find me when I thought Annie had died in Nam. With a broken heart and Americas miserable treatment of Vietnam vets returning home I was riding into the mountain wilderness. I desperately needed to get away from civilization and everyone in the human race. It was Sam Young, whose expert assistance gave Annie the information she needed to find me before I disappeared from life.

Lieutenant Coldwater said "I'm going to miss him too. It's sad he wasn't able to enjoy some of his hard

SEARCH FOR ANNIE

earned retirement. He recruited me into this business, treated me like I was his son, he will be terribly missed." The three of us stood by as Tim Walker and Henry Steel with several commandos walked by carrying the stretcher with Sam Young's body on it. They walked past us to the medivac and lifted Sam Young's body on board, placing it beside General Mueller or, aka, Henry Tuttle, British Agent with MI-6. After a few moments of self-thought and deep respect we watched the chopper lift off and fly north until it disappeared from site.

Lieutenant Coldwater turned to Annie and said "I do have some good news."

"And what would that be Lieutenant?" Annie asked.

"We have JP over here on our chopper with all the care he can stand."

Annie and I ran over to the chopper and picked up JP in our arms. We felt a great burden of relief come over us as we realized we were now a family again. We climbed aboard the chopper and started to fasten our seat belts when we heard a loud roar emanating from inside the hangar. In a flash it dawned on me we had forgotten about the missile. Hilda's last instructions, to her techs, were to set the missile on automatic countdown to fire. Sam and I raced from the chopper toward the hangar. People were racing out of the hangar as fast as their legs could carry them.

I yelled "IS THERE ANYONE STILL INSIDE?"

One of the commandos running by turned to me and hollered out "NO SIR, I'm the last one out!"

Just as Sam and I reached the hangar the missile fired off. The shock wave from the blast, created from the engine exhaust, blew out some of the corrugated metal panels along with a couple of doors. It knocked Sam and I backward, about ten feet, slamming us to the ground. We quickly lifted ourselves up and backed away from the hangar as fast as our legs could carry us. I watched the missile clear its launching pad and fly northwest out of site. Sam radioed in the missile launch to the command post, but N.O.R.A.D. had already been alerted to its launch and scrambled two F-16s out of San Diego. The F-16s were carrying heat seeking missiles. Fortunately they were able to shoot it down over the southwestern Arizona desert near a wildlife refuge where the population was non-existent. Lieutenant Sam and I climbed aboard our chopper and strapped ourselves in to our seats. I sat next to Annie who was holding JP. When the chopper lifted off I took one last look at the smoking hangar. I knew how fortunate we were to have survived what could have been a terrible disaster for us. There were so many more people who weren't aware of the danger that could have had their lives destroyed. This entire crisis happened because a handful of psycho's wanted revenge.

Chapter XXI

Several weeks have passed since the kidnapping and missile firing. It was nearly Thanksgiving and Annie and I had a lot to be thankful for. Thank God our air power was able to shoot the missile down before it did any damage. Annie, JP, and I have been staying with Jim and Mary while they were healing from their wounds. Mary, Annie and I attended Sam Young's funeral in Washington D.C. Several hundred people were there to pay their respects. He was laid to rest with full honors at Arlington National Cemetery. It was a sad time for all of us, especially Jim and Mary who had known Sam Young for over thirty years. Jim wasn't healthy enough yet to travel and felt bad he couldn't attend but everyone understood why. Annie and I haven't been able to bring ourselves to visit our destroyed home yet, but our neighbors and friends have been taking care of the ranch livestock during our absence. Annie and I had been finding all kinds of excuses not to go home.

Four weeks after we had returned to Colorado, Mary started asking us when we were going to return home and start rebuilding again. She kept telling us it wasn't good to take advantage of our friends and we needed to face up to our troubles and overcome them.

I told her "Our neighbors were caring for the animals. Other than that there was nothing we could go back to until we made sure she and Jim could take care of each other."

Mary replied "I think you two and JP need to go home and start your lives again. Jim and I are healthy enough now to care for ourselves."

Annie looked at me and said "She's right Cody, we need to go rebuild our home and give JP a place to live."

"Ok sweetheart, we'll go out there early in the morning and start getting estimates on what it will cost us to rebuild."

The next morning the sun was shining brightly but the temperature felt like it was near forty degrees. Annie, JP and I climbed into our pick-up and headed home for our ranch in La Jara. The Aspen trees were losing their bright yellow colored leaves and the mountains around us were covered with snow. We turned right onto our dirt road in La Jara and headed west. When we drove through Centro and passed the barn I had been hiding behind when all the trouble had started, my memories returned along with all the terror that took place. I looked at Annie who was looking at me with those beautiful blue eyes. She smiled and said, "It's over sweetheart. Let it go."

I looked at JP who was sleeping peacefully in his car seat we had strapped down between Annie and I. Looking at both of them I thought to myself, *'I'm the luckiest man alive.'*

As we approached our house, or what we thought would be left of it. We noticed a-half dozen cars were parked in our drive. What totally shocked us was to see a newly constructed home that was just about completed. Annie and I were stunned as we looked at each other and wondered who had done this and why would they do it on land they didn't own?

We pulled into our drive, Annie got JP out of his car seat and we both exited the truck feeling a bit shocked at all that was going on. We started to approach the house when we saw Sam Coldwater come out the door wearing a carpenter's apron.

He spotted us and hollered out "It's about time you two showed up. If you would have waited one more week we probably would have had it completed."

When we walked up to him he turned toward the house and hollered in "HEY GUY'S SARGE IS HERE WITH HIS FAMILY!"

That's when the biggest surprise of my life

happened. The last two members of my remaining recon team, Tom and JJ, walked out of the house with their hammers and wearing nailing aprons. JJ was walking with an artificial foot which he received after stepping on a booby trap. It happened during his tour in Nam while we were on patrol just outside Tay-Ninh. Tom was still the quiet shy young man from Ohio who apparently completed his Nam tour without a scratch.

I asked with surprise "What in the world are you guys doing here?"

Tom replied "Sam called us and told us what had happened to your family so we all came here to help you and Annie rebuild."

Then Tom turned to Annie and said "Miss Anne it's good to see you again. I'm glad you made it back alive."

JJ stepped down off the porch with a sneaky grin on his face. He said "When Sam returned from that mission in Mexico he told us what you and Annie had been through. So we figured since we had nothing to tie us down for a while, we all agreed to come down here and help out our old "Sarge" and his lovely wife and son. Everyone in town pitched in and helped with supplies and labor. Annie's parents provided the money that was needed. That's how we were able to complete it so quickly. Consider this a gift from your friends and family.

JJ looked over at Annie and with deep respect in his voice said "Miss Anne, I personally want to thank you for all you did for me. When I was in your M.A.S.H unit back in Nam I learned if it wasn't for the good care you gave me I might have also lost part of my leg. Now, if you three are ready, we'd like to show all of you, your new home?"

Before Annie, JP, and I stepped up onto the front porch to follow our friends into our new home I held JP and Annie tightly in my arms. I wondered what I would have done if we hadn't all, been able to get back alive. I looked into Annie's beautiful blue eyes and kissed her softly on the lips. I then looked up into the clear blue sky and said "Thank you GOD for these friends."

We stepped up onto the new porch and Annie went in first with JP. I started to enter the door when Sam stopped me and motioned for me to step back out with him. I followed his lead until we were far enough away from everyone so he could speak privately.

Sam looked at me and said "While we were going through the belongings of all the dead I happened to come across something I thought might be of interest to you. I was searching everything Hilda Mueller had in her possession and found this."

Sam handed me a woman's beautiful broach and when I saw it my heart started racing so fast I thought I was going to have a heart attack.

I said "This looks like a broach my mother use to wear."

Sam replied "I believe it is your mothers. If you look on the back you'll see the initials EM with a heart and then the initial PM which, I believe, stands for Elizabeth Miller, your mother and Paul Miller, your father. If you open the broach you'll find a picture of some young boy about four years old. Is it you?"

I unsnapped the broach case and opened it up. Shock set in and Sam had me sit down on a sawhorse that was standing close by. I couldn't believe it, I just couldn't believe it, after all these years I finally have a new lead that might help me find my father and mother.

I asked "Was there anything else?

Sam said "Only this. I found it tucked in with your picture" He handed me a small piece of folded paper.

I opened the paper and found, inside, some faded numbers with several letters. I looked up at Sam and said "This could be co-ordinance."

Sam hesitated for a minute and looked as if he was being tormented by something. I looked up at him and said "What else is troubling you Sam?"

He hesitated a while longer but finally said with a solemn tone "We identified all the bodies in the hangar except one."

A shudder passed through my body, as I asked him "Who's missing?"

Sam replied "Herman Kessler."

Sam continued "We have no idea how he may have gotten away. The only thing we can figure is he was able to slip away during the shootout under the cover of all the gun smoke and confusion going on inside the hangar. We have him listed on the ten most wanted and Interpol wants him too."

I heard a noise behind me and turned to see Annie standing there with JP.

Sam looked at Annie and said "Miss Anne, I don't believe he will ever be back. If he's still alive, we will find him, I promise."

I got off the sawhorse I was sitting on and walked over to Annie. I could see the concerned look in her eyes as I put my arms around her and walked with her around to the back porch. We stood there in silence for a few minutes watching our two mules and our Appaloosa grazing in the pasture nearby. The cool air blowing at us from the beautiful, snowcapped, mountains surrounding our ranch gave us the feeling of calm, serene, and peaceful life.

I looked at Annie holding JP and said "Life will always have its troubles for us to face. We have come through several already and there probably will be more for us to come. As long as we have each other nothing and no one will ever destroy the powerful love we have for each other."

Just before we turned to join our friends in our new home, Annie looked at me and said "I love you Cody Miller and I want you to know one more thing."

I asked "What would that be?"

Annie smiled at me and said "You're going to be a father again."

The End